A FROZEN SILENCE

Deputies Frack Tilsley and Robely Danner are called to a remote section of woods outside their small farming community of Abundance, Wisconsin, where a man stands handcuffed and frozen to a tree. As they investigate this brutal murder, a young woman discovers the purse of a missing secretary from nearby Promontory which contains a cryptic diary. Digging deeper, Tilsley and Danner discover common denominators linking several suspects to two murder victims and possibly a third, with the chief of police himself on their list . . .

ARLETTE LEES

A FROZEN SILENCE

Complete and Unabridged

LINFORD
Leicester

First published in Great Britain

First Linford Edition
published 2017

A catalogue record for this book is available
from the British Library.

ISBN 978–1–4448–3132–0

Published by
F. A. Thorpe (Publishing)
Anstey, Leicestershire

Set by Words & Graphics Ltd.
Anstey, Leicestershire
Printed and bound in Great Britain by
T. J. International Ltd., Padstow, Cornwall

This book is printed on acid-free paper

1

Fire!

Smoke weaves through Rosalie's dream. She's twelve years old, roasting marshmallows over the bonfire at summer camp. Her twin sister Sylvia is there too, both of them slender and tan as long-distance runners. They got along in those days, sneaked out one night to the Boy Scout camp where a full moon hung like a Chinese lantern above the lake. They smoked their first cigarette with a couple of cute young guys, did a little innocent kissing and made it back before dawn without getting caught. They did a lot of things in those days without getting caught, and later, a few things that weren't that innocent.

Smoke from the campfire brings tears to Rosalie's eyes. She circles the stones but the smoke follows her. The other girls laugh with delight, wondering what magic allows Rosalie to bend smoke to her will. She's in her element, the center of attention, with Sylvia sitting quietly on the sidelines.

She coughs. Her eyes open. Rain pounds the roof of Lovelace House, the big Victorian on Euclid Street. She's twenty-two, not twelve anymore, and something isn't right.

'Sylvia?' She snaps on the lamp. Her sister's bed is empty. She remembers now. The last time she saw her she was standing on a desolate stretch of road, her car in the ditch. Rosalie drove away laughing in her cozy Volkswagen, leaving Sylvia standing in the rain.

It doesn't seem half so funny now that Rosalie has sobered up.

A burning smell fills the room. It irritates her throat. She coughs. Her landlady should be asleep, but that doesn't mean she hasn't left something scorching on the stove. Miss Jennie is in her 60s, usually lucid, except when she calls her dog, Woofie, who died years and years ago.

There's a crackling sound like a cat

playing inside a paper bag. A tendril of smoke crawls beneath the door from the landing. She jumps up and races across the room. The brass doorknob singes her fingers and an arrow of panic shoots across her chest.

'Marlis! Wake up!'

Marlis is the third roommate, the one Miss Jennie calls the sensible one. Rosalie shakes her and the young woman opens a reluctant eye.

'What?' she mumbles. 'What, for god's sake? Don't you know what I've just been through?'

'Get up! The house is on fire.'

2

Black Ice

Three weeks before the fire.

Rain taps against the windowpane. It's a perfect morning for sleeping in while the dying coals flicker in the fireplace. Frack and I, along with Big Mike Oxenburg, are deputy sheriffs at the small substation in Abundance, Wisconsin. If it wasn't our day off, we'd be patrolling Little Papoose Lake, ordering fishing shacks off the ice before it breaks up for the season.

Frank 'Frack' Tilsley and I live in unwedded bliss in a cream-colored Victorian overlooking the town square. In summer it's lush with grass, its maples and oaks heavily leafed, grey squirrels tumbling through the branches like acrobats on a caffeine high. But this is March, and you get whatever mother nature dishes out.

Frack opens his eyes and rolls toward me. He's a whippy chain-smoker who picked up his nickname working oil-fracking operations in North Dakota. After a stint in the marines, he moved back to Abundance, a farming village with one stop sign, two churches, and three bars, one owned by my mother, Gladys Calhoun.

I'm Robely Danner, pronounced ROW-blee, as in row, row, row your boat. I was five years on the force when Frack signed on. He has extensive firearms experience, while I've only fired my service revolver twice in the line of duty, once to dispatch a wounded buck and again when a rabid raccoon invaded the mayor's chicken coop. I made the front page of the local paper, which is approximately the size of a church bulletin.

Our dog Fargo commandeers half the bed, the middle half. Last year I found him abandoned along the highway and took him home. He's big and fluffy, a little clumsy and always hungry. He licks my cheek and I ruffle his ears.

Frack leans toward me. I rise on an

elbow and meet him halfway for a morning kiss. 'Fargo, off the bed,' I command.

He studies me with wounded eyes. *Me? You can't possibly mean me.*

'Now,' I say, gently but firmly. He lies down in front of the fireplace with his chin on the Raggedy Ann doll he got for Christmas.

The phone jumps to life. I groan. 'Don't answer it. It's going to be you-know-who.'

'Could be an emergency — a cow on the highway; a lost gas cap. Hello.' He listens briefly and covers the mouthpiece with his hand. 'It's her. She's been drinking.'

'I told you,' I mouth, thumping back on the pillow.

Gladys Calhoun has been a familiar name in law enforcement circles since before I was born. My four-times married and divorced mother seems to have wed every man she's slept with except the father of her only child . . . me. I heard my dad was a French-Canadian, a lumberjack with two fingers missing on his left hand. Gladys refuses to divulge his name, and my birth certificate is no help. It reads 'Father: Unknown.' She gave me her maiden name, Danning, and kept her last husband's . . . or was it second to last? Gladys dumped the Frenchman soon after I was born. He wanted her to stop sleeping around and driving drunk with me in the car. If you know Gladys Calhoun, you know that's asking too much.

I've avoided Gladys's calls since I moved out of the apartment above the bar with Fargo. The bar is located in the mosquito zone above the Little Papoose River. The green neon beer sign in the window is the first landmark you see when you turn off the main highway into town. The fact that I don't take her calls doesn't mean I don't love her. I just don't want to be around her. There's a difference . . . I think. It's a long story that runs through my childhood like a rusty razor blade.

'Tell her I'm not home,' I mouth.

'She says it's an emergency.'

'Isn't it always?'

'It's early, Gladys. I'll tell her you called when she wakes up.' He clicks off without waiting for a response and moves the phone to the night stand.

We settle in bed with newspapers and coffee, listen to the rain and lounge in the warm quilts. Frack taps a cigarette from his pack and snaps a flame from his Ronson. His hands are strong and callused, working man's hands that repair furniture and rescue deer that have fallen through the river ice. I'm addicted to his nicotine kisses and how his smoky scent blends with the smell of pine when he comes in from the woods behind the house. Gladys says my father carried the same scent in his wool shirts . . . well, the guy she *thinks* is my father. Thanks, Gladys. You're a real gem.

'Anything interesting in the Chicago paper?' I ask.

'The usual.'

'Here's a good one,' I say. 'A van transporting fifty silver fox coats from Elan Fashion Furs in Minneapolis is overdue on its Chicago run. The driver, David Dorne Coburn, delivered ten coats to a department store in Wausau, then vanished, truck and all.'

'I wonder what coats like that are worth?'

'Plenty, I'd imagine.'

We read everything of interest and toss the papers on the floor. Frack pulls me against his side. Rain blows against the window. A log collapses on the grate and sends a shower of sparks up the chimney. The moment I toss my nightgown aside, the phone rings.

'The best laid plans . . . ' he says.

I reach across his chest and grab the phone, engaging in a brief conversation with a lot of okays and yeses coming from my end. 'At least it wasn't Gladys,' I say, clicking off. 'Remember Jennie Lovelace?'

'The retired teacher out on Euclid.'

'It's about a missing lawn ornament. It's been in her family for fifty years.'

'You mean that ugly cement leprechaun by her bird bath?'

'It's a gnome,' I say.

'What's the difference? It's a midget in a pointy hat.'

'Leprechauns are Irish. The gnome is

Bavarian. He has a big nose, one foot on a log, and an ax in his hand.'

'Sounds like a mean little sucker.'

'Miss Jennie doesn't drive in the rain. She wants us to pick up a photo of the stolen item and run off some flyers. She's offering a twenty-five-dollar reward for its return.'

'I guess we could go by in the morning.'

'She said at our earliest convenience — provided it's today.'

'That does it!' Frack tickles my ribs, tosses back the covers and gets out of bed. 'Come on. I'm taking you to breakfast.'

Breakfast means the Bluebird, the only café in town. After pancakes and coffee, we head to the car, where Fargo snores contentedly in the back seat. The rain has morphed to snow, the windshield wipers brushing away the slush. The radio warns of a blizzard blowing down from Ontario.

'Just what we need,' I say. 'More snow.'

The town, which had a population of 5,000 in its lumber-rich days, has dwindled to less than 1,000 souls, the mill on the river gone the way of the movie house and Five and Dime. There are 'For Rent' signs in several windows along the one-block business district, the result of a crippled economy and a Walmart in a nearby town that challenges local establishments with rock-bottom prices.

Even a small town has a right and wrong side of the tracks. Once Main Street passes over the abandoned railroad spur, we're on the wrong side. To our left is Bubba's Biker Bar, with its greasy parking lot. A few adjacent houses are abandoned, others for sale to get a jump on foreclosure.

We turn right on Euclid at the outer edge of town and drive another half mile until we come to a muddy one-lane called No Name Road. It leads back from Euclid to a trailer park with its adjacent field of gutted sofas and non-op cars.

On two acres at the corner of No Name and Euclid is the once-elegant Lovelace House, with its historic carriage house and giant oak trees. On a sunny summer day, when its carefully tended flower gardens are in bloom, there's a whisper of grandeur about its sweeping veranda and second-story cupola. In winter it sits proud but paintless, a ragged orphan begging a crust of bread.

★   ★   ★

In the big stone mansion on the rich end of the lake, Claudine du Lac Bratton throws the newspaper across the breakfast table, tipping over her husband's orange juice. 'Would you please keep our names out of the newspaper? How many times do I have to say it?'

The kitchen maid rushes over with a tea towel and dabs at the tablecloth. 'Thank you, Tippy,' says Will.

'Is there anything else I can . . . ?'

'You can go away,' says Claudine.

'Yes, ma'am.'

'It's an article about the flying club,' says Will. 'What's the harm in that?'

'Can't you see they only use you to drag my name into print?' Claudine snatches the paper and turns to 'People In The News.'

'Husband of former Claudine du Lac, heiress to the du Lac granite fortune, stands next to his vintage 1955 Piper Apache PA-23 . . . blah, blah, blah,' she reads aloud. 'Mr. and Mrs. Bratton married one month after the tragic death of her parents in the crash of their private plane . . . Show me once where they mention your name. Can't you see that it's just a way to drag the same old incident into print?'

'Do you think I'm not equally annoyed at being 'the husband of'?'

'Ever hear the expression, 'You better be careful what you ask for'?' The beautiful woman in her twenties studies the bull-necked, beer-bellied man in his early forties and finds him sorely lacking in all the social graces the du Lacs are so well known for.

'We can still make this work if you'd only let it,' he says.

She finishes her coffee and lights a cigarette. 'I hope you're getting your tax mess in order,' she says more quietly. 'I don't want it ending up in my lap.'

'I've hired a CPA now that Ruth is gone.'

'What's her name?'

'Marlis Underhill. She's very capable.'

'Hear from Al's widow?'

'Not since Al passed away. I don't think Julie will press ahead with a lawsuit.'

'Good.' Claudine looks out the window, lost in a world of her own thoughts.

'Claudine?' he says. 'Let's try to make the best of our situation.'

She gives him a look that could cut paper. 'This is as good as it gets.'

★   ★   ★

Jennie Lovelace opens the door before we knock. She's small-boned and sharp-eyed, with grey hair pulled into a bun. 'No uniforms?' she says, checking out my old jeans and Frack's vintage pea coat.

'It's our day off, ma'am. If you like, we'll go change into something more official,' I tell her.

'Don't bother.' She squints at me over her bifocals.

'You're Robely, Gladys Calhoun's girl.'

'Yes, I was here a few weeks ago when the branch went through your attic window. Don't you remember?'

'Of course I do. I taught you in fifth grade. You haven't turned out half bad . . . considering. I always knew you'd end up a cop or a criminal.'

'It wasn't an easy decision, ma'am.'

'You say a cement leprechaun is missing?' says Frack, coming to my rescue.

'It's a *gnome*! A Black Forest woodcutter. And when cement hardens it's concrete, not cement. Wipe your feet and come in. I just had the carpets cleaned.'

We step into a broad central hallway, stairs going up on the right, the left side leading to an outside door at the back of the house. Twin girls in their late teens or early twenties come bouncing down the stairs and out the door.

'You remember Rosalie and Sylvia Dearborn,' says Miss Jennie.

'Yes,' I say. 'They're very pretty girls.'

'They look like angels, except for their

shoulder tattoos. Did you know one of them shoplifts?'

'That hasn't come to my attention, ma'am.'

'I won't say which one. I figure she'll get caught or outgrow it. My third tenant was gone when you came before. Marlis Underhill. She's the reliable one, a licensed CPA.' As we talk, she ushers us through a large archway into the parlor. She motions us to matching easy chairs and sits on the loveseat across from us.

Despite the house's sad exterior, the inside is elegant and well kept. There are crown moldings, Oriental carpets, and old family portraits on the papered walls. Lovelace had once been the centerpiece of a large agricultural holding, most of which was parceled off during the Great Depression. Miss Jennie has never gotten over the loss of land, even though most of it was gone by the time she was born. The trailer park sprang up where the Lovelace barn once stood, which aggravates her no end.

'Here's the photo of Mr. Holzheimer,' she says, handing Frack a snapshot. 'I took that picture when the snapdragons were in bloom. I want flyers posted all over town. I can't say conclusively that it was taken by a delinquent from the trailer park, but nothing ever went missing until those welfare people dragged their trailers into that mud hole at the end of No Name Road.'

★   ★   ★

Rosalie and Sylvia walk toward the carriage house where the cars are parked. They have pale green eyes, winter-white complexions, and dark hair blunt-cut at the shoulder like Egyptian princesses. They wear stylish fur-trimmed boots and matching red coats, snowflakes swirling around their heads. Empty horse stalls and old harnesses line the walls, and toward the back a buckboard sits beneath the dust of decades. High above their heads, hundreds of bats hang like velvety black fruit from the lofty belfry. Rosalie opens the passenger door of her Volkswagen and Sylvia walks toward her Cruiser.

'I thought we were taking my car,' says Rosalie.

'I'm not in the mood for shopping today.'

'How about a movie?'

'I don't think so.' Sylvia reaches for the door handle.

'But we had plans.'

'I know,' says Sylvia.

'What's that supposed to mean?'

'It means I'm meeting Kent Longtree at the Bluebird. You can come along if you want to.'

'You mean tag along like the family dog?' says Rosalie, advancing a step or two. The color is already rising to her cheeks.

'I have to go. Let's talk later.'

'Oh, please indulge me with an explanation, Your Majesty.' She pokes her sister in the collarbone with a gloved finger.

'Don't touch me!'

Rosalie opens her purse, taps a Virginia Slim from the pack, and lights it with her Zippo. She inhales deeply and blows the smoke out through her nostrils, then closes the lighter with a snap and drops it back in her purse. She looks like a petulant child who's stolen her mother's cigarettes. She also looks dangerous. The twins are the mirror image of one another: high cheekbones, long eyelashes, and baby-doll noses. Most people can't tell them apart, except for Rosalie's flashes of temper.

'All right, calm down,' says Sylvia. 'I can't shop with you anymore. I don't want to be there when you're busted for shoplifting.'

'Like you've never nicked a lipstick here and there?' She takes another pull from her cigarette, aggressively blowing out the smoke.

'Getting caught at twenty-two isn't the same as getting caught at twelve. Your name would be in the paper. Small-town people have long memories. Besides, why steal something you can afford to buy?'

'Who are you to interrogate me? You're not my mother. You're not even my friend.'

'Oh, for crissake! Grow up.' Sylvia turns and walks toward her car.

Rosalie grabs the shoulder of her coat and spins her around.

'Do not put your hands on me.'

'I bet you think Kent Longtree is wrapped around your little finger.'

'He's asked me to marry him, if that's what you mean.' She'd hoped for a more opportune moment to make the announcement, but now it's out.

A tremor of insecurity ripples up Rosalie's spine. 'You didn't say yes?'

'I did. Why shouldn't I?'

Rosalie teeters on the crumbling edge between rage and tears. 'Does he know about all the sleeping around you did before he came along?' she says vindictively.

'You mean that *we* did? I've put that in the past long ago.'

Rosalie shoulders into her. Sylvia smells her sister's perfume, the tobacco on her breath, her incandescent rage. She's never known anyone who can flip so quickly between one emotion and another. 'I've heard all about Kent Longtree. He's quite the stud. He'll dump you for the first piece of trash who comes down the pike. When he does, don't come running to me, because *I don't care!*'

Sylvia's hand lands on the side of Rosalie's face with a resounding clap. Rosalie staggers sideways, her cigarette landing in the dust ten feet away. 'Spoiled brat!' shouts Sylvia. 'You're never happy unless you make someone else as miserable as you are.'

Rosalie is stunned. She touches the red welts on her cheek.

The front door opens and closes. The deputies start their car and drive off. Sylvia climbs in the Cruiser, slams the door and clicks down the locks. Her sister pounds her fist on the window and twists a kink in the aerial. Sylvia looks straight ahead. The engine turns over and the Cruiser rolls slowly out of the carriage house. As it reaches the street, Rosalie picks up an old horseshoe and runs after it. She pitches it at the car but it falls short.

'I'll get you for this!' She punches the air with her fist, slips on a patch of black ice, and lands painfully on her hip. Tears blur her vision as the car disappears down Euclid Street.

Miss Jennie shakes her head and lets the parlor curtain fall back in place.

★　★　★

In a bar in Appleton, owner Joe Vittoni watches a man slide onto the stool beside Phyllis McCoy. She sits against the wall furthest from the door, her thoughts turned deeply inward. Phyllis is a trim woman with a poodle-head of penny-gold curls, bright orange fingernail polish and a bracelet jingling with charms — not a bad looker for someone in her forties. The man is about to deliver his pickup line when she nails him with a stare as frosty as her gimlet. When he walks away, she thumps her purse on the empty stool and picks a Camel from her pack.

Joe leans over the bar with a light. 'I've never seen you this quiet, Phyllis. You usually come through the door like a Kansas twister.'

'Ruth is missing.' A tear sparks the corner of one eye. 'She left work over two weeks ago and vanished into thin air.'

'The last time I saw her, she was here with you.'

'Let me know if you hear something.'

'You betcha.'

★   ★   ★

'So, where to?' says Frack as we drive back toward the center of town. Fargo gives a little yip as he chases rabbits in his sleep. The snow comes down in earnest, feathering the sidewalks, the windshield wipers turned up a notch.

'We could go to the station and run off the flyers,' I say.

'Mr. Holzheimer can wait a day. Anything else come to mind?'

'Oh god, you can't mean Gladys.'

'The longer you put it off, the harder it's going to be.'

'I don't want to be dragged into her b.s. again.'

'Come on, kid. You have to give her credit for what she does best, and b.s. tops the list.' I can't help laughing. 'Whose side are you on?'

'Maybe she simply misses you.'

''Simple' is not a word I associate with Gladys Calhoun.'

'Well?'

'All right, but let's make it brief.'

We drift through the business district and cross the Little Papoose. It's thickly wooded between the river and the main highway. An unfamiliar patrol car pulls out from behind a concealing cluster of pine trees and waves an old Dodge onto the shoulder.

'What the hell!' says Frack. 'He's not one of us.'

'That car was going twenty miles an hour.'

Frack pulls over and eases to a stop. The cop has his ticket book in hand when we get out of the car. He's wearing a white Stetson and cowboy boots. *Wah hoo! He must think he's John Wayne,* Robely muses wryly. He raps on the side of the Dodge and the window rolls down.

'Turn off your engine and show me your driver's license,' he says. The driver complies. The farmer behind the wheel is

83-year-old Grover Gunderson.

'You were going ten miles over the limit.'

Frack and I do a slow burn.

'This car is twenty-five years old,' says Gunderson. 'It can't go the limit, and I've got a twenty for anyone who can prove otherwise.'

'That's just the number I have in mind,' says the cop. 'It could make this problem disappear like the hair on your head.'

'I didn't have a problem before you came along.'

'You've got a real mouth on you for an old goat.'

We come up behind the officer. 'What's going on?' I say. 'I know this man.'

'Get back in the car, both of you.'

'This is an illegal stop. You were hidden from view.'

'Who the hell are you to tell me my business?'

I flash my shield. 'I'm Deputy Danner. This is Deputy Tilsley. And you are?'

'Promontory's newly elected chief of police, Burgess Bratton,' he says, puffing out his chest. He's neckless and beer-bellied, with a case of pungent b.o.

Frack walks over and leans into Mr. Gunderson's window. 'Hi, Grover.'

'Hi, Frank.'

'Go on home. This little game is over.'

'He tried to squeeze me for a twenty, Frank.'

'I heard him. Put your wallet away. And thank Gracie for the blackberry jam.'

'What the hell are you doing?' says Bratton as Mr. Gunderson drives off.

'Protecting and serving. You're out of your jurisdiction, Chief.'

He looks at us with eyes as hard as bullets, walks to his car, and stuffs his big hard belly behind the steering wheel. Then he turns onto the highway and disappears around a bend.

'I hope we've seen the last of him,' I say. 'His breath could kill a buffalo at twenty paces.'

I tie my red muffler to the tree where Burgess Bratton had been lying in wait. It's my signal for Tree Toppers to cut the branches back.

*　*　*

The split-log siding of Gladys's Bar comes into view. A one-ton pickup truck with a bald rear tire is parked in the lot. We pull in beside it and get out. In the bed is a load of firewood. A hand-painted sign says, 'Seasoned Oak. Neighborly Rates.'

'Neighborly rates?' I say.

We pass beneath a rack of caribou antlers tacked above the bar entrance. The interior hasn't changed since I was a kid. The walls are hung with deer trophies, antique firearms and Fox Indian artifacts. A Worlitzer bubbles red and blue against a side wall. At night the place comes alive with the ding of a 1940s pinball machine, the click of billiard balls, and the cha-chunk of cigarette packs tumbling into the tray.

Gladys sits behind the bar with a beer next to her morning coffee and a cigarette smoked down to the filter. A purple bruise blossoms across her cheekbone, and her left index finger is bandaged.

'Hi Mom.'

'Hi, baby.'

Frack gives her a nod. 'How you doing, Gladys?'

'Same old, same old.' She shrugs, crushing the butt of her cigarette in an ashtray from the Ho-Chunk Casino. She's dressed in black leather jeans, a tank top with a Harley-Davidson logo, and silver skull earrings. My mother is in her early 50s but looks 65. She has dyed red hair and a complexion pickled and smoked from decades of alcohol and cigarette use. That doesn't mean that a certain kind of man — like the four she married and divorced — doesn't find her husky voice and pre-cancerous cough irresistibly sexy. Despite her vices, she maintains a trim figure and hard sinewy arms. She keeps a baseball bat behind the bar and a Derringer in the cash drawer, and is proficient in the use of both.

'It's been a while,' says Gladys.

'The job keeps me hopping,' I say, taking the stool across from her.

'I can imagine,' she says. 'No uniform today?'

'We're off the roster.'

Frack takes the stool beside me.

'Anyone want coffee or an eye-opener?' she asks.

'I'm fine,' says Frack.

'Me too,' I say.

'Where's the moose?'

'Fargo? He's sleeping in the car.'

'I've never known such a useless animal. All he does is sleep and eat.'

'Sounds like your third husband.'

Gladys laughs and picks a shred of tobacco from her lip. 'You got a quick tongue.'

'So, how's business?' says Frack.

'Good. Same old crowd, although I see too many familiar faces in the obits these days. Time marches on. What can you do?'

We spend the next fifteen minutes in small talk. Finally Frack says, 'So what's with the truck outside? You in the market for firewood at neighborly rates?'

'Sleeping Beauty is upstairs. I want him back on the road.'

'He give you trouble?'

She touches the side of her face. 'You mean the bruise? He's a restless sleeper.

The finger I caught in a cabinet door.'

Gladys is a tomb of denial. If you hooked her to a polygraph, she'd melt the wiring.

'This Romeo got a name?'

'Dick . . . no . . . Nick Vanderhoot. He's down from the Upper Peninsula.'

'Michigan then. Known him long?' I ask.

Gladys cuts me a jaded glance. 'It was a long night, if that's what you mean.'

I look at Frack. 'Let's check out the truck. I want to know who we're dealing with.'

We head for the parking lot while Gladys works on her coffee. Fargo is awake and smiling at the car window. I let him out to explore the woods along the river.

Frack writes down the license number. The truck is locked, so I get the Slim-Jim out of the trunk, slide it inside the door next to the window, and unlock it.

'This probably isn't legal,' says Frack. 'No probable cause.'

'How about the bruise on Gladys's face?'

'I'm good with that.'

There's a chainsaw the size of a motorcycle behind the front seat. I rifle through the glove compartment and produce a one-ounce bag of weed. 'You got a problem with this?' I ask.

Frack shakes his head.

'Me neither.' I toss it back. We find no weapons and lock up.

Fargo is back from his romp with enough snow on his nose to make a snowball. He waits until he gets in the car to shake his coat, then lies down and goes back to sleep.

'Ready?' says Frack.

'Let's do it.'

I don't like walking to the floor above the bar. I stop outside the room that used to be mine. It's being used to store cases of liquor and broken bar stools. Memories flood back like a grainy reel from an old movie.

The year is unclear. I wake in the night. Gladys is passed out in her room. Her latest one-night stand comes down the hall and steals into my room. A hand claps over my mouth. If I make a sound he says he'll burn the place down. After a few traumatic minutes, he leaves and walks down the hall to the bathroom.

I run to Gladys's room and shake her awake. She reeks of whiskey. Mascara is smeared beneath her eyes. She doesn't like what I have to say. 'You mention this to anybody, I mean anybody, they'll lock you in the nuthouse and throw away the key.'

I become an angry distrustful child who sleeps with a chair wedged beneath the doorknob. I lose weight. I have nightmares. I'm afraid to speak in front of the class. Miss Jennie asks if there's something I'd like to tell her. I shake my head. I don't want to go to the nuthouse.

Frack knows my story. He squeezes my shoulder. 'Ready?'

'Can't wait.'

★   ★   ★

Miss Jennie sits at the desk, at war with her checkbook. No matter how many times she reworks her figures, they refuse to balance with the bank statement. The

32

front door opens and slams shut. She turns her head in time to see a whirlwind fly up the stairs. Marlis Underhill presses against the banister to let Rosalie pass, then pokes her head into the parlor.

'Is Rosalie okay?' she asks.

'She's a complicated girl,' says Miss Jennie. 'Come on in.' Marlis is tall, with auburn hair and blue eyes, a classic beauty in her Burberry coat, leather briefcase in hand. 'Off to work?'

'That's the story of my life. After I'm through at Bratton's, I'm renting office space and hanging out my own shingle.'

'With all the empty storefronts on Main Street, you should be able to swing a reasonable lease.'

'I hope so. Looks like you're into a book-keeping project of your own.'

'I've gone over my figures a dozen times,' says Miss Jennie, 'and I'm still short $112.'

'You mean this month, or every month?'

'Every month for over a year.'

'That's a loss of $1,344 per annum,'

she says, effortlessly doing the math in her head.

'I can't figure out where I'm off.'

'Just put it aside for now. I'll get back to you in a few days and we'll figure it out.'

★ ★ ★

Rosalie wipes her tears and tosses her snow boots into the closet, where they land with a thud. She peels down to her slip, rubs her bruised hip, and flops onto the bed. She touches the welts on her cheek. It's always been Sylvia and Rosalie, Rosalie and Sylvia. Now some guy wants to shoehorn in between them.

Last fall, Kent Longtree shot the biggest wild turkey of the season and got his picture on the front page of the paper. Tall. Curly hair. Big smile. All the girls went nuts over him. Any guy who's that popular is going to fool around. It's in the DNA. All she has to do is prove it to Sylvia so things can go back the way they used to be.

Frack and I follow heroic snoring to Gladys's bedroom. Vanderhoot is sleeping with his mouth open and one leg hanging off the bed. He's big and bearded, with long hair and a necklace of red and blue beads, a cross between Paul Bunyon and Timothy Leary.

I pick his overalls off the floor and pull out his wallet. The man's full name is Nicholas John Vanderhoot, Iron Mountain, Michigan. DOB 4-6-72. Hair: Brown. Eyes: Brown. Height: 6′ 3″. Weight: 245. He's carrying two hundred dollars in various denominations. I flip though the plastic pockets: Visa card, library card, and the snapshot of a cute strawberry blonde leading a little boy on a spotted pony. I put the wallet back and nudge the mattress with my knee.

'Nick.'

Nothing

Another nudge. A groan. An empty gin bottle rattles across the floor.

'Get up. Time for a cigarette.'

A bloodshot eye opens. He squints at

Frack and me. 'Who are you?'

'Your friendly neighborhood cops,' says Frack.

Nick swings his feet to the floor. He's wearing a wife-beater T-shirt and Betty Boop undershorts. After a shower and a trip to the dog groomer, he'd be a pretty good-looking guy.

'I'm Danner and this is Tilsley,' I tell him.

'I'm here by invitation of the establishment,' he says.

'Check-out time is ten a.m.'

'Very funny.'

Frack tosses him his overalls and plaid Pendleton. Nick stumbles into his clothes. He pulls on his socks, then grabs his steel-toed boots and laces them up. He yawns and lights a crippled Lucky.

'I notice you're hauling a load of wood,' says Frack.

'It's for my girlfriend's wood store, but I can sell you a half cord real cheap.'

'That where you're headed?'

'Yes. She lives on the family farm outside Promontory.'

'The one with the little blond boy?' says Frack.

Nick snorts a laugh. 'You've been through my stuff.'

'What's her name?'

'Nancy Jackson.' I write down the address. 'We met at the Lumberjack World Championships in Hayward. She does amateur log rolling and I placed in men's single bucksaw. Next July we're competing in the Jack and Jill bucksaw event.'

'You log for a living then?'

'Yeah, both me and my dad, until he got cut in half when the chain busted on his saw. The mortician had his hands full trying to put the pieces back together for the viewing. He wanted to charge me extra.'

My stomach does a slow roll. 'You have anything to do with the bruises on Gladys's face?' I ask.

'What bruises?' He looks genuinely oblivious.

'You have outstanding warrants, Mr. Vanderhoot?'

'No.'

'A record?' I press him.

'An old DUI is all. How come you two are out of uniform? Is this casual Friday or what?'

'It's our day off,' I say. 'If it weren't for you, we'd be in bed reading the funny papers. The next time you see the cut-off to Abundance, keep going. And stay away from Gladys Calhoun.'

'You mean I can't even stop for a beer?'

'That's right. She's trouble with a capital T.'

'How can you say that?'

'I've known her a long time. She's my mother.'

★ ★ ★

Halfway between Abundance and Promontory is Bratton Moving and Storage. The operation sits on two flat acres surrounded by a chain-link fence. Marlis parks in the long open-fronted garage, where small moving vans are sheltered along with employees' cars and miscellaneous equipment. Adjacent to the garage are two parallel buildings each housing 20 storage units, with locks hanging from their aluminum roll-up doors.

When Marlis gets out of her car, Rommel, a gentle young Doberman, comes to greet her, wagging his stubby tail. 'That's my good boy,' she says. His deep bark alone is enough to discourage midnight fence-jumpers.

Hank Logan, one of the movers, hops down from his pickup. He's young and lean, with a coiled intensity that draws women like an industrial magnet. He has shiny brown hair that falls to his shoulders. His resemblance to James Dean is uncanny. The other mover, an older man named Benny Goddard, says Bull and Hank don't get along; but Hank's his nephew, so he's stuck with him.

Rommel jumps with excitement as Hank tosses him a sausage biscuit, a daily ritual the dog looks forward to.

'Morning, Miss Underhill.'

'Good morning, Hank. You sure have a way with dogs.'

'I have a way with a lot of things,' he says, with a smile that looks like an invitation to a roadside motel.

'Well, have a good day.'

The building closest to the road contains three office units with exterior doors facing into the yard. The first is the reception area. Marlis has the middle office, and the third is Bratton's cave, where he watches videos with an excess of squeaking bed springs and heavy breathing.

When Marlis enters her office, there's a note in red felt pen on top of her computer. *I quit. Good luck. Missy Fisher*. 'Oh no,' she says.

The door opens and Will Bratton walks in. The man is round-faced and carries an extra hundred pounds in all the wrong places. 'Missy's late,' he says.

She hands him the note without comment.

'If she thinks she's going to collect unemployment, she's got another thing coming. How about you? Making progress?'

In the corner of the room is a grocery bag containing financial documents thrown together in a jumble.

'It's going to take time to get your documents in order,' Marlis says.

'Just make it look good for the auditors. How hard can that be?'

'It has to *be* good. It can't just *look* good. That's why you're in this mess.'

'I want you back here tonight. From now on you put in a full eight hours.'

'In that case I'll need the gate key.'

He slides one of two matching keys off his ring and slaps it onto her desk. 'Don't lose it,' he says.

'One more thing, Mr. Bratton. I was hired part-time. Those extra hours are going to show up on my time sheet.'

'Whatever,' he says, and walks out the door.

Marlis empties the bag on her desk and starts organizing the contents. At five, when everyone leaves for the day, she takes a dinner break in town and has duplicate keys made at the hardware store.

★ ★ ★

Kent is 24 years old, the official catch of Waupaca County. After the Bluebird, he

41

and Sylvia drive to Promontory and take in a double feature.

It's dark outside when the show is over, and they step into a dense swirl of snow. They run to the car through the pink and purple lights from the marquee.

As soon as they buckle up, Kent's cell phone rings. He talks for a few seconds and then clicks off. 'Shorty needs help with the dinner crowd,' he says. 'Do you mind coming with me to the Bar and Grill? You can go upstairs and watch TV until I'm through working. I'll drive you back to your car when the weather lightens up.'

Sylvia readily agrees. Anything is better than facing Rosalie.

When Kent's father died, he inherited Longtree's and moved into the apartment above the restaurant. Business is better now than when his father was alive. Kent has a bigger smile. He shoots bigger turkeys. He's got an inexhaustible gift of gab.

'I'd like that,' she says.

They pull onto the main highway. The pavement is as slippery as glass, and the woods on either side labor under the weight of snow. Directly ahead, a truck carrying a load of wood is stranded on the roadside with a flat.

'He'll never get a tow truck out here in this weather,' says Kent as the truck disappears in his rearview mirror.

Longtree's Bar and Grill backs onto Lost Squaw Creek, the picture window in the dining room overlooking a frozen tableau of delicate white birches. Dinner is served between seven and ten, and the first customers are pulling into the lot.

Kent and Sylvia push into an anteroom containing a cigarette machine and a newspaper rack. They're about to go into the main dining room when a fiery-haired young woman with a hobo bag slung over her shoulder bolts past them, elbowing Sylvia against the cigarette machine.

'Ruby! Where the hell are you going?' says Kent.

With eyes straight ahead and mouth set in a hard line, Ruby straight-arms through the outer door, climbs into her car, and fishtails onto the highway.

'Are you all right?' Kent asks.

'Just startled. That was your server, wasn't it?'

'Yes. Let's find out what's going on.'

Shorty is true to his name, a former jockey about 50 years old, five foot two, 112 pounds. On the counter beside the freezer is a small mountain of silver-plate serving utensils.

'Glad you're here, Boss,' he says. 'Hi Sylvie, my dear.'

'Hi Shorty.'

'What's up with Ruby?' asks Kent.

'She almost got away with the soup ladle. When she dropped it, I stopped her and found the mother lode in her bag. You want I should call the sheriff?'

'Let me think it over,' says Kent, as their first customers come through the door.

Meals are buffet-style, a set menu for each night of the week, except Monday when they're closed. Tonight it's sizzling brats on a sourdough bun with a side of chili. Kent takes his station at the cash register and Shorty mans the spigots.

A lady takes a sandwich from the stack. She stops and looks at Sylvia. Sylvia automatically grabs a ladle and fills her bowl. For the next few hours customers trickle in, about half the usual number due to the storm. Sylvia helps a man through the door in his wheelchair, wipes up kid's soda spills, fills coffee cups, and talks weather and crops. If you can't talk weather and crops, they make you leave the state. When she finally looks up, the diners are gone and the doors are locked. Shorty starts the dishwasher, gives a wave, and heads out the back exit to his car.

Sylvia turns to Kent, who wraps his arms around her and kisses the top of her head. 'My feet have never been so sore,' she says. 'What happened to watching TV?'

'Come on. I'll rub your feet. I didn't mean for you to get stuck like that.'

'Oh please,' she says as they head up the stairs. 'I know a setup when I see one.'

Kent turns the radio on low. The weatherman predicts 15 inches of snow by morning. He looks out the window into a world of furious white. 'There's no getting back to town tonight,' he says.

'I hadn't planned on going back,' she says.

When he turns around, Sylvia is stretched across the bed in her slip, her shiny black hair fanned out across the pillow. 'I've never been on a water bed,' she says, creating a gentle wave with her hand. 'I thought they went out with sex, drugs, and rock and roll.'

'This is the last one on the planet. The seller threw in the lava lamp for a buck. And for your information, sex and rock and roll are still around.'

'I guess I was misinformed.'

He sits at the foot of the bed. 'How does that feel?' He kneads one small sore foot, then the other.

'Like heaven.' A few beats pass in silence. 'I bet you can make me feel even better.'

He studies her expression with a thoughtful pause. 'I bet I can. You know, we've been together for four months now. You know all about my dad and his struggle with cancer, and my mom dying when I was little, but you never mention your family.' She opens her mouth to speak. 'No.' He holds up a finger. 'Your dad is in jail and your mom is chained in the attic like Mr. Rochester's mad wife.'

'It's nothing half so interesting. My parents are divorced. My mom runs a gourmet wine and cheese shop in Green Bay. I worked there every summer when I was growing up. I can name fifteen varieties of cheese in five seconds. After high school I wanted to try something new, so I moved to Abundance. I have an unmarried cousin named Luisa who owns a fabulous inn in Manitowish.'

'What about your father?'

'Del? We don't talk about him.'

'A story for another day, then. You never let me pick you up at your place. Why is that? It's always at the Bluebird or the library or the town square, like we're spies or adulterers. You're not hiding a husband somewhere, are you? I've been down that road and it's full of bumps.'

'My landlady is a bit finicky about male visitors, but she's really very nice.' Now would be the time to tell him about Rosalie, but why ruin the mood?

'The sooner we get married, the better,'

says Kent. 'I see no point in waiting till June, do you?'

'Let me think about it.'

'You can have a permanent job at the restaurant. It pays more than unemployment, and you won't get laid off like you did at the library.'

'What about Ruby?'

'She won't be back after today. Listen, Sylvia, the customers loved you tonight. Don't overthink it. Just say yes.'

'Okay, yes.'

'Yes, to what?' he teases, tickling the bottom of her foot.

'To you, to the Bar and Grill, to everything.'

'Everything?'

He moves up beside her and kisses the butterfly tattoo on her right shoulder.

3

Into the Night

Rosalie zigzags over the hazardous back roads as the white-out becomes a full-blown blizzard. All day she's vacillated between rage and tears, hormones mixing in her blood like an unstable chemical experiment. If Sylvia can get a steady guy, she can too, except he won't be some curly-headed kid who shot the biggest turkey of the season. He'll have money and substance.

Up ahead, loops of gold neon spell 'Cloud Rest Motel and Café.' She slows to a crawl. She has no idea where she is. Across the road from the motel is a bar called Dowling's. Out front are two Fords, three pickup trucks and a shiny new Lincoln.

Rosalie parks and goes inside. The men at the bar turn their heads as she slides out of her faux-leopard coat and hangs it on the rack inside the door. She wears black velvet jeans, a silver-sequined top, and boots with stiletto heels, bringing her to a full 5′ 5″. Through veils of cigarette smoke they watch her fluff snowflakes from her hair. It doesn't take a bloodhound to detect the lethal level of testosterone in the air.

Where to sit? Not by the man in the ball cap, the farmer in work boots, or the mechanic in blue overalls. An older man in a black business suit sits alone in a booth against the wall, quietly stirring his drink. The Lincoln has to be his. Beside him is a briefcase topped with a handsome white-banded fedora. She can't remember the last time she saw a man's hat without sweat stains on the band. She gives him the hint of a smile. He gives a barely perceptible nod of the head. She crosses the room and sits in the booth across from him.

'I hope you don't mind,' she says. 'If I sit at the bar I'll be devoured by wolves.'

'I'm Larry Jordan,' he says, offering his hand. He has an ordinary mid-fiftyish face, dark blond hair silvering at the temples, and thick-lensed dark glasses. She tries not to look at the heavy black mole above his left eyebrow.

'Rosalie Dearborn.'

'That's a lovely name.' Her hand is small, with pink nails. She smells young and sweet, like baby powder and cotton candy.

'I've never seen so many candles,' she says, looking around the room.

'It's in case the power goes out. Would you care for a drink, Rosalie — something to take off the chill?'

'Mexican coffee would be nice.'

Larry nods to the bartender. Dowling walks over. 'She'll have a Mexican coffee. Another whiskey sour for me.'

'I'll have to see I.D.'

'Mine or hers?' says Larry. All three of them laugh.

'The young lady looks sixteen,' says the bartender.

Rosalie produces her driver's license and Dowling delivers the drinks. 'Keep the change,' says Larry, handing him a twenty.

'You're not from around here, are you?' says Rosalie.

'How can you tell?'

'No hayseeds in your hair. No cow muck on your shoes.'

'I'm passing through. Do you have plans for the evening?'

'I did when I started out, but I lost my way. Do you always wear dark glasses at night?'

'I have migraines. Light bothers my eyes.' Larry relaxes with his drink and sizes her up. She's the kind of woman men take advantage of and the kind of woman who lets them.

She looks out the window. A flurry of snowflakes turns gold in the halo of the motel sign. 'I think we're snowed in until morning, don't you?'

'Probably. I have a room at the Cloud Rest for the night. Would you care to join me, or would you rather howl with the wolves until morning?'

Rosalie finishes her drink and picks up her sequined purse.

If a fox could smile, he'd look like Larry. He knew how the evening would end when she walked through the door. By the time she joined him, he'd already dropped his wedding ring in the pocket beside his Saturday night special.

★ ★ ★

Marlis pulls off the highway. It's dark, snow piling against the chain-link fence. The gate stands open, the lock with the red stripe across its face gone. When she parks outside her office, Rommel isn't there to greet her.

There's a different feeling out here at night, like the last train has left the station and you're alone on the empty platform. When she gets out of the car, the cold shocks her lungs. She fumbles for her inhaler and forces a few shaky breaths in and out.

Inside the office, she locks the door behind her. She switches on the overhead and the light in the outside corridor. Looking in the mirror behind her desk, she tames her wind-blown hair and settles behind her computer. Next she dials Mr. Bratton's home phone. A woman answers.

'Mrs. Bratton?'

'Yes, this is Claudine.'

'This is Marlis Underhill at the storage facility. Is Mr. Bratton in?'

'He's addressing the Knights of Columbus down at St. Pat's.'

'When he comes in, please tell him that the gates were open when I arrived and I don't see Rommel anywhere. I don't feel safe walking out back to investigate.'

'Nor should you. I'll send someone out and let Wilbur know when he comes in.' It's hard to think of her boss as Wilbur, when everyone at the yard calls him Bull. 'I'm glad you've taken the job,' she continues. 'Since Albert fell ill, the books have been a mess, and my husband has no acumen for mathematical detail. I thought Miss Chambers was competent enough, but I haven't seen her since the day she quit. With Albert gone . . . oh well, I won't bore you. I'll tell Will you called.'

'Thank you, Mrs. Bratton.'

'It's just Claudine. I'll have you to the house for lunch one day soon.'

'Thank you, I'd like that,' says Marlis,

terminating the call.

Who's Albert? She spins through the Rolodex and finds Missy Fisher's number.

'Hello.'

'Missy, it's Marlis. I got your note.'

'I knew you'd call. I didn't want to quit with Bull there. You've never seen him in one of his rages, but stay long enough and you will.'

'Any chance I can talk you into coming back for a few weeks?'

'With the price of gas being so high, Daddy insists I take a job in town.'

'I'll miss you. I just spoke with Mrs. Bratton. She sounds young. Mr. Bratton must be in his forties.'

'She's twenty-something, a real looker. She's the one with all the money in the family.'

'That's interesting.'

'I mean, Bull has money, but not *that* kind of money. Have you seen the house they call Chateau du Lac?'

'Only from a distance. It's the stone mansion on Little Papoose Lake.'

'Claudine inherited the place when her parents died. We had the office party there one year. There's a huge wine cellar and freezers full of game. There must be five hundred bottles of wine, not that I'd know a good year from a bad.'

'She mentioned someone named Albert.'

'Albert Paxton? He was Bull's partner. He died on Christmas night after a prolonged illness.'

'How sad. Claudine told me he used to do the books?'

'Bull mostly ran the storage end while Albert handled the finances. The last six months before he passed, he was in a wheelchair, always in and out of the hospital. That's when Ruth Chambers took over. A few weeks before you signed on, she up and left. When I asked Bull about it, he just grunted. Mr. Eloquence.'

Marlis laughs. 'Has the partnership been audited before?'

'I don't know. I was only here for two of the eight years he and Al had been in partnership. I was hired right out of high school.'

'What did Mr. Paxton die of?'

'An intestinal thing. I thought it was

cancer, but Claudine said it was something called Crohn's Disease.'

They talk a while longer and then click off. Marlis opens the computer and begins entering data. After hours in the same position, she stands and works the kinks from her back. As she studies her tired face in the mirror, a red eye of light appears in the glass. She looks around the room, but doesn't see the origin of the reflection. It reminds her of the red beams that target people in adventure movies.

She turns off the overhead, returns to the mirror, and stares into the cold surface. She runs her hand over the cold glass. The spark is gone. All she sees is her own shadowy image. She turns the light back on and looks at her watch. It's eleven p.m. From now on she'll work a full day, but she's not coming back at night.

She gathers her things and locks up. The snow is driven by a stiff wind. She hears a faint sound, stops beneath the overhang, and listens. She walks to the door of Bull's cave. 'Anyone there?' No reply. No light leaks from the edge of the blinds, but she hears a slight scratching noise, perhaps a whine.

'Rommel?' she says. She tries the knob. The door is locked. A tree branch scrapes against the roof and a waterfall of snow tumbles onto her shoulders. She shudders and brushes off her coat. The moment she gets in the car, she clicks down the locks.

Claudine must have asked PPD to do a security check, because a patrol car pulls into the yard as she pulls out. Visibility is down to fifteen feet, maybe less, as she heads for home. If she drives too slowly, she might be rear-ended. If she speeds up, she could rear-end a car in front of her. She never should have come out here in the first place.

Bull Bratton rises from the leather recliner in his cave and snaps on a lamp. He sets his extinguished cigar in the ashtray, takes a riding crop from a hook on the wall, and raises his arm. The whip whistles through the air and Rommel gives a sharp yelp of pain.

'When I say quiet, I mean quiet.'

Nick Vanderhoot is stuck on the side of the road with a flat. He wants to call Nancy, but he's left his phone at the bar. If that Gladys woman hadn't come onto him like a succubus, he'd be in a warm bed at the farm by now.

He polishes off a bag of Doritos, wraps himself in a blanket, and lies down on the seat, contorting his body to accommodate the stick shift and steering wheel.

Sometime before dawn, he dreams that a thundering 18-wheeler is bearing down on him. He wakes with a terrified whoop and hits his head on the underside of the dash.

★ ★ ★

Rosalie kicks off her shoes and lies back on the motel bed. 'So what do you do, Larry? It must be important. Nobody around here wears a suit unless it's to a funeral.'

'I sell drugs.'

'You don't look like a drug dealer.

Where's your black hoodie? Where's your beeper?'

Larry laughs and sits on the edge of the bed. 'I work for a pharmaceutical company.' He mentions the name. She's seen their commercials on TV. 'I visit doctor's offices, give them samples, and take their orders. I cover a lot of territory. The road gets terribly lonely.'

'I know what that's like. I'm lonely all the time. What's in the briefcase? Samples?'

'You're a smart lady.'

She puts her arms behind her head and her sparkly top creeps up a few inches.

'What about you, Rosalie? You must have a good job to pay for all those pretty sequins. I bet you work in a jewelry store or behind a perfume counter.'

'I worked — past tense — in a flower shop, just long enough to get unemployment. Then I made them fire me.'

'How did you do that?'

She rises on an elbow. 'A man ordered a dozen red roses for his mistress. The card read, 'For My Intoxicating Sherry,

Your Pooh Bear.' He tucked a hundred-dollar bill among the leaves. I had it delivered to his home address. His wife kept the money and got rid of Pooh Bear. He came back to the flower shop and punched my boss in the eye.'

'You're a very inventive person.' A velvet strap slips off of her shoulder, drawing his attention to her unicorn tattoo. It's a delicate work of art. So is she. 'Let's have a nightcap,' he says.

'No more alcohol for me.'

'I have something better.' He finds plastic cups in the bathroom and removes the cellophane wrappers, then fills them from a thermos, drops a crushed pill in one, and watches it dissolve. He brings the drinks back to the bed and hands her one.

'Hot chocolate,' she says, sitting up. 'You're so sweet, Larry. You're not married, are you? I'll be broken-hearted if you say yes.'

'I was once, but she died years ago.'

'We're going to see one another again, aren't we?'

'I live a long way from here.'

'But you pass through. Maybe you could take me with you sometime.'

'I'll give you my cell phone number. We'll work something out.'

'That's wonderful. This isn't something I'd normally do — spend the night with a stranger, I mean.'

'I'd rather you saw me as a friend,' he says, the light reflecting off his thick lenses.

'Oh, I do.' She finishes her drink and lies back on the pillow. Larry takes the cup from her hand. Her eyelashes flutter softly. 'I'm spinning like a top. I shouldn't have had that drink at Dowling's.' She covers her mouth with her hand and yawns. 'There are two of you, Larry. There was only one of you a minute ago.'

'You just need to rest your eyes.'

'Am I dreaming, or is this real? You seem so far away.'

'I'm right here. Let yourself drift.' By the time the words are out of his mouth she's under and won't come around for hours. He walks over and opens his case. Everything is there: handcuffs, duct tape, black garbage bags. The only drug Larry carries is Rohypnol.

★   ★   ★

It's almost midnight when Jennie wakes to unsettling silence. She gets out of bed and puts on her robe, then opens the door and steps onto the veranda. The snow comes down at a slant.

'Woofie!' she calls, but the wind drives her back inside. 'Where can he be? He used to come when I called.'

She climbs the stairs and puts her ear to the attic door, then peeks inside. All the beds are empty. She looks at the boarded window and reminds herself to get it fixed. Next she walks to the second-floor guest room and peers out of the window overlooking the back garden. Snow is piled like sheep's wool in the frozen flower beds.

A man stands behind the carriage house this side of No Name Road. She pushes up the window, letting in a blast of cold air. Even in the dark she senses they're making eye contact. He's probably a drunk staggering home from the biker bar.

'Get off my property you bum,' she yells, 'and don't you dare pee in my snow.' She blinks and the shadow is gone. As she slams the window shut, the door opens behind her and she spins around with a gasp, hand over her heart. Marlis is standing there with briefcase in hand.

'Marlis, for god's sake! You scared the life out of me.'

'I thought I heard a noise. No one ever comes in here.'

'At least one of you ladies is home safely.'

4

Into the Frozen Woods

Sunlight flares through the windshield, putting an end to the most miserable night Nick has ever endured. The storm has blown over. He drags himself to a sitting position, his foot coming alive with a million needles, the muscles in his back a tangle of knots.

A snowplow flies by, dumping three feet of snow against the side of his truck. He flips off the driver and receives a cheerful blast of the horn. He'd give himself more time to wake up, except for the urgent need to relieve himself. He climbs, stiff-legged, out of the truck and through the ditch into the woods.

After accomplishing his mission, he looks around. Except for his footprints and the yellow spot he left at the trunk of a tree, the snow is pristine. Ice silvers the branches overhead, and he takes a moment to enjoy the tranquility, then plods deeper into the trees. His foot stops tingling. The knots in his back loosen their grip.

He's about to turn back when he sees something strangely out of place in the near distance. It looks like a snow-covered yeti hugging a tree. Curious, he circles at a distance. He whistles, but the thing doesn't respond. He moves closer. When he's at arm's length, the yeti becomes a man whose handcuffed hands are looped over a branch a foot above his head. He reaches out. The body is stiff, wisps of blond hair peeking from beneath a wool cap.

'Holy Christ!'

Nick brushes snow from beneath the cap. The face is turned his way, the mouth gaping in a silent scream, terrified blue eyes staring at him through a lens of ice. He gives a full-throated holler and stumbles backward. He doesn't remember running through the trees or jumping the ditch. The driver who stopped on the road says that Nick was standing on the yellow line, waving his arms like a windmill in a hurricane.

★   ★   ★

Rosalie is dreaming. She's sixteen, living with her family in Green Bay . . .

She waits until her parents are asleep, then climbs out of the bedroom window. A breeze whispers through the treetops as she runs the five blocks to the river. Becky called around dinnertime. She wants to be friends again. After Rosalie won the gold medal in the Regional Spelling Bee, Becky slapped it out of her hands and ran off stage crying.

A big summer moon floats on the surface of the river, broken into golden fragments by the swift current. Rosalie inches her way down the bank beside the bridge. A pebble lodges in her sandal and she shakes it loose. Except for the rush of water, it's very still.

'Becky?' she says. 'It's Rosalie.' No answer. It's black beneath the bridge. She hears the scraping of shoes against stones and a boy steps into the moonlight. It's Rocky, Becky's older brother, the dropout

67

and town troublemaker.

'Where's Becky?'

'I came instead.'

Her fear is immediate. 'That wasn't the deal.' She turns to leave, but Rocky blocks her path.

'Becky studied hard for that competition,' he says.

'So did I.'

'You embarrassed her in front of all those people.'

'She's a sore loser. She embarrassed herself.'

Rosalie pushes him hard and starts up the bank. He's right behind her, dragging her back down. She's heard about the things he does to girls and starts to cry. He spins her around and grabs the front of her dress. A button flies off. A seam rips. He grabs the hair on both sides of her head, and with the sour taste of wine on his breath, forces a rough kiss on her lips. She jabs blindly at his face, by sheer luck her thumbnail plunging into his left eye socket. He yells and covers his face with his hands, a thread of blood oozing between his fingers. When he can see again, Rosalie is gone.

As soon as she climbs back in the window, the light snaps on. Her father stands in the doorway, slapping the feared wooden spoon against his thigh. He takes one look at her disheveled appearance and accuses her of going all the way with a boy. She tries to explain, but once Del Dearborn makes up his mind, nothing can change it. Her mother stands with her hands crossed over her chest.

'Mom, help me!' Without a word her mother turns away and leaves the room.

Before Sylvia can drag him off of her, Rosalie's legs are covered in raw welts. It's the worst of many whippings she's received at his hands. Sylvia is now seen as the good twin and Rosalie the bad one.

The next day Del packs his bags and never returns. Her mother cries for days and blames Rosalie for ruining the family. Her grades go from As to Ds and she does all the things she's been accused of and more. After they graduate, she and Sylvia catch the Greyhound and ride until their money runs out. Sylvia closes the door on the past, but Rosalie carries her scars everywhere she goes.

Rosalie wakes, feeling dizzy and feverish. Someone is knocking on the door. She falls getting out of bed, and struggles to her feet. 'Yes?' she says, cracking the door an inch.

'Housekeeping, ma'am. Twenty minutes to check-out.'

'Yes, thank you.' Her thoughts come slowly into focus. She looks around the room. Larry is gone. The briefcase is gone, as are the plastic cups and cellophane wrappers. Rosalie may be foolish, but she's not stupid. The hot chocolate had been drugged. The room looks as if Larry Jordan was never here. After all his efforts, she finds herself untouched and wholly intact. It's all very confusing. She returns the room key to the desk clerk, whose name tag reads 'Fay.'

'Have you seen Mr. Jordan this morning?' Rosalie asks.

'He left about twenty minutes after you arrived. Mr. Dowling helped dig his car out.' Fay hands her an envelope. 'He left this for you.'

Rosalie rips it open. *Received an urgent message from the home office. Sorry for the sudden change of plan.* He'd left her forty dollars for breakfast and gas, but no phone number. If you can't trust a man in a Lincoln, who can you trust?

'Where am I?'

'Deer Springs,' says Fay. 'Population, fifty-eight. Don't look so disappointed. It could be worse.'

'What do you mean?'

'Mr. Jordan could have been the Traveling Butcher.'

'The what?'

'The guy who's been killing all those women, brunettes like you. He's never offed a blonde as far as anyone knows. Then again, they haven't found all of the heads, so who can say?'

* * *

By the time we wake, the storm has blown east over Lake Michigan. Frack and I are up early papering the downtown with Mr. Holzheimer's ugly mug. The snowplows are clearing the streets, merchants shoveling their sidewalks.

There were so many collisions, spin-outs and snowbound cars that tow trucks are coming in from outlying towns. Back at the station, every phone line is blinking. As Big Mike finishes one call, another line lights up. Frack and I start punching buttons. The calls go something like this:

When will the snow plow reach Birch Street?

A stray cow is standing on our porch.

A tree has fallen on our roof.

My mother just slipped on the ice and broke her arm.

I call for the first responders and pick up the next call. 'Deputy Danner. How may I help you?'

'Hi, Robely. This is Oscar Philbrick.' Everyone knows Oscar. He owns the feed store. 'I was driving toward town when a man waved me down. He says there's a guy handcuffed to a tree in the woods.'

'Did you say handcuffed to a tree?' Frack and Mike look up and I motion for them to listen in.

'That's what he told me. He says he's

fifty yards or so beyond the ditch'.

'Alive?'

'He doesn't think so.'

'Can you give me a landmark?'

'Cross the Little Papoose and turn right on the highway. Drive ten miles and pull up behind a truck with a load of wood and a flat rear tire.'

'Thanks, Oscar. We're on our way.' I click off.

Frack and I look at one another. 'That truck sounds mighty familiar,' he says.

I shake my head. 'Say it ain't so.'

We turn to Big Mike, our superior officer. He sprained his ankle getting out of the car this morning and can barely make it to the coffee and donuts, although he manages.

'Go, you two,' he says, 'but keep me posted. What do you bet it's a scarecrow?'

*   *   *

Marlis weaves between the stranded cars on her way to work. Bratton is on site and Hank Logan is piling snow against the back fence with the John Deere.

She pulls her car into the space beside Bull's yellow Cadillac. When she gets out, Rommel crawls from beneath one of the vehicles. With his head down, he sidles over and presses against her knee. She kneels down to his level. 'What's wrong, boy?' He looks up but the spark is gone from his eyes. 'You come with me,' she says. He limps along behind her, holding up his right front paw. She's reminded of the open gate and wonders if he's gone into the road.

She enters her office and closes the door behind her, Rommel clinging to her side. She tosses her coat and briefcase on the chair, kneels down, and runs a hand gently over the dog's back. There's swelling along his spine and ribs. He gives a little yelp of complaint.

'You poor boy,' she says. He licks her hand. His gums are pale, his nose dry. She finds an old coat in the closet and spreads it in front of the heater. He limps in a circle and lies down. By the time she settles in with her paperwork, he's asleep.

Marlis picks up the copy of last year's filing, the one being challenged by the

IRS. Several deductions appear legitimate — roof repairs, mileage, and vehicle upkeep. Several others don't pass the smell test. She puts her coat back on and finds Bratton arguing with Hank between the storage buildings. Hank walks off as she approaches.

'What now?' says Bull.

'We need to eliminate a few deductions. That way I can get you through the process in half the time.'

'What deductions?'

'Donovan's Liquors, for instance. Cigars. Adult films. Really, Mr. Bratton. What were you thinking?'

'I was entertaining clients.'

'The IRS is capable of closing your business if you try to cheat them.'

'If I lose deductions, it's going to cost me.'

'Cheating the IRS will cost you more. There are a few other items we have to address.'

'Like what?'

'Swede's Snowmobiles. Lakeside Jet Skis.'

'Never heard of them. They must have

been Al's purchases.'

A dying man? I find that highly unlikely, but don't bother arguing the point. 'Since you and Al were partners during the year in question, you are jointly and severally responsible for any accrued indebtedness. You're a businessman. You know what those words mean.'

'If you were a man, you wouldn't let them push you around like this,' he says.

'*You're* a man, Mr. Bratton. How's that working for you?'

'All right, do what you have to, Miss Underhill.'

'Did you find out what happened with the gate last night?'

'Don't worry about it.'

'One more thing. Rommel has been injured. I'd like to — '

'I don't want to hear about it. I'm shopping for a real guard dog.' He turns and walks away.

'Mr. Bratton?' He doesn't look back. 'Mr. Bratton!'

★ ★ ★

Nick Vanderhoot is leaning against the tailgate of his truck when Frack and I get out of the car. 'Looks like you've been rode hard and put up wet,' says Frack.

'I'm not used to looking at dead people before my first cigarette.'

'Are you covered for towing?' I ask.

'I am, but my phone is back at Gladys's.'

'No one would have come last night anyway. Tell us about the man in the woods, then we'll concentrate on getting you back on the road.'

'Just follow my footprints.'

'What time did you discover him?' asks Frack.

'As the sun came up.'

'What inspiration took you into the woods?'

'A full bladder.'

'That'll do it. Was the man warm or cold?' I ask.

'Stiff as a side of beef, ma'am.'

Frack and I wade through the ditch. The snow is deep and falls into my boots. We follow Nick's trail until we're ten feet from the body. One thing is clear: it is not a scarecrow. We stand in the frozen silence, surrounded by purple shadows broken by patches of crushed-diamond snow. If it weren't for the corpse at center stage, it would make a lovely Christmas card.

'Ready for a closer look?' says Frack.

'I was born ready.'

As we examine the corpse at close range, terror-stricken eyes stare at us through a coating of clear ice. The man's mouth gapes wide and ape-like, the entire face contorted against the rough bark.

Maybe I'm not as ready as I thought.

We circle the tree and I snap pictures from all angles with my camera-phone. The forensic photographer will take a set of official photos for the coroner's file, but these are for the Murder Book.

I turn to Frack. 'Have you ever seen . . . ?'

'No. I'm sure I'd remember.' Hand-cuffs are looped over a four-inch branch that holds the corpse upright. 'I wonder how long he's been here.'

'The only footprints are Vanderhoot's

and ours, so he would have been here before the blizzard. Beyond that, it's like looking into a freezer and guessing how long the ham has been frozen.'

'What about age?' says Frack. 'I'm figuring mid-thirties.'

'Whatever it is, The Iceman is as old as he's ever going to get. We need Sheriff Brooker and Paula over here.' Paula Dennison being the county medical examiner.

'The Iceman?' Frack says.

'We could call him The Snowman, like Frosty, but it sounds a bit too cheery, don't you think?'

'He could be the missing driver. The one we read about in the paper.'

'Then where's his truck?'

'Maybe it was towed. I'll make a few calls. If you want to get Vanderhoot's phone, I'll call Paula and tape off the scene while you're gone,' he says.

'That works for me. Give Mike a call too.'

Back at the road, I take Vanderhoot's statement. 'I'm going to Gladys's to get your phone. Wanna come?'

'I'd rather stay here and freeze to death.'

I reach into the patrol car. 'Catch,' I say. 'I hope you like brats and horseradish on sourdough.' My sack lunch sails through the air and Vanderhoot catches it with the enthusiasm of a hungry wolf.

★　★　★

Along the back wall of Marlis's office is a filing cabinet she has yet to explore. The top drawer holds a lunchbox containing a mummified apple and a bottle of antacid tablets. In the center drawer is a first-aid kit and old newspapers.

Marlis kneels beside the bottom drawer and pulls out a sweater and a quality leather purse. Inside is a wallet. The name on the driver's license reads: 'Ruth Ann Chambers, 754 Delaware Street, Promontory, Wisconsin. DOB: 10-17-64. Hair: Light Brown. Eyes: Brown. Height: 5′ 1″. Weight: 98 lbs.' The photo is that of an attractive, intelligent-looking woman with stylish hair cropped like a 1920s flapper. In the bill compartment is $140. There's also a diary, an address book, makeup, and the usual miscellaneous items. If this is the woman Missy said quit, what is her purse doing here?

She hears footsteps in the corridor, shoves the purse back in the drawer and slams it shut. Bratton walks in on a cold gust of wind and closes the door. When he crosses the room, the dog trembles and gives Marlis an imploring look more eloquent than words. A shiver ripples down her spine. She gets to her feet and brushes dust from her grey slacks.

'Making progress, Miss Underhill?'

'I'm checking the filing cabinet to make sure I haven't missed anything.' She looks at her wristwatch. 'I have to go. I'm having lunch in Promontory.'

'As long as you're back in an hour. Time is money, Miss Underhill.'

Marlis can't wait to get off the lot. She knows a woman keeps her purse with her whether she goes to the powder room or outer space. She'd never leave her money or her most personal items behind — at least not voluntarily. She puts Miss Chambers's purse inside her briefcase and snaps it shut, then pulls her car around to the door. Next she tries to coax Rommel onto the back seat, but he looks at her and whines, too injured to jump and too heavy for her to lift.

Benny Goddard sees her dilemma and walks over. 'Let me give you a hand.' He picks up the dog in a way that causes the least pain and settles him carefully on the back seat.

'These injuries are no accident,' she says, in a whisper. 'I'm taking him to the vet.'

'That's good.' Benny stands there as if he has more to say.

'What is it?' she asks.

'Your office,' he says in a low voice. 'Watch what you — ' He cuts his sentence short, gives her hand a squeeze and walks off. Bull is watching them from the office window.

She gets in the car and swings through the gate onto the highway.

★　★　★

Larry Jordan speeds southeast between frozen pastures and cornfields ragged with stubble. Even with the visor pulled down and his prescription sunglasses in place, the glare off the snow is like a flashbulb exploding in his face. There's no way to describe migraine pain unless you've had a corkscrew twisted into your skull.

He can't stop thinking about Rosalie. He'd had her right where he'd wanted her — drugged, helpless, and all to himself — but he'd never touched her. With his murder kit open, he was still unable to act. Her face was too vulnerable, too tenderly angelic, her thin patina of sophistication an unconvincing masquerade. She wasn't like those other whiskey-faced dames who needed their heads cut off. A couple nights ago he'd tried to force a drunken hag into his trunk. She'd jabbed him with a hatpin and gotten away. He's in a panic. It's the first time the prey had seen his face and lived.

★   ★   ★

83

The day after the attempted kidnapping, 30-year-old Florence Dooley worked with a police sketch artist in a Milwaukee precinct. She's a barfly and sometime hooker who says a man grabbed her when she exited the alley door of Porky's Bar. She hates the cops and wouldn't be here unless he'd shaken her to the core.

The artist works patiently until the drawing is complete — well, almost complete. Something's missing. She'd only seen his face for a panic-filled second, but she closes her eyes and brings the moment into focus.

'He has an ugly black mole the size of a dime above his left eyebrow. If he was a john, I'd have charged him extra,' she says with a broken-toothed grin.

★ ★ ★

Rommel stands shivering on the stainless-steel exam table, wary of the strange surroundings and the man in the white coat. 'What happened to this dog?' asks Dr. Alderman.

'I believe he's been beaten.'

'You don't know?'

'He belongs to my boss. He doesn't know I'm here.'

'Who do you work for?'

'Will Bratton, at the Moving and Storage.'

'Secretary?'

'CPA. I'll be hanging out my shingle as soon as I find office space.'

'In Promontory?'

'Probably Abundance, but I'm not sure yet.'

'There's a gift shop going out of business up the block. The owner will be looking for another tenant in a couple weeks.'

'Thanks, I'll keep that in mind.'

As they talk, Dr. Alderman is running his hands over Rommel's coat, feeling his bruises, speculating about his joints. Rommel flinches and gives a low growl. 'I'm sorry, boy. I know that hurts.' He turns back to Marlis. 'His spine is bruised. I think at least two, maybe three ribs are broken, and his paw is broken or badly sprained. We'll need X-rays to see the extent of the damage. Do you know if he's had his shots?'

'I don't know his medical history. He was purchased as a guard dog, but Rommel wants to be a sixty-pound lap dog instead. I don't want to return him. Do I have to?'

'Let me work on that from my end. Okay?'

'Okay.'

'I'll put him on pain medication tonight. Call me tomorrow. I'll know more by then.'

Marlis signs the financial responsibility form. She puts a hand on either side of Rommel's face and kisses him lightly on top of the head. 'I'll be back,' she whispers in his ear. 'Thank you for everything, Dr. Alderman.'

'Call me Mark. My mother does.' That gets a laugh, and he smiles. He's a tall, personable man somewhere in his forties, more Gregory Peck than Sylvester Stallone. Marlis finds him warmly compassionate and very appealing.

'And you can call me Marlis,' she says, extending her hand. As their fingers touch, a little jolt of electricity jumps the synapse between them. 'Sorry. It's the dry weather.'

'It could also be something else,' he says, playfully wiggling an eyebrow.

Marlis walks to the car with an irrepressible smile on her face. She's been gone an hour and ten minutes and still hasn't had lunch. *Time is money, Miss Underhill.* Her thoughts turn to Ruth Chambers and the emptiness in her stomach. Bull Bratton will have to wait. If she's lucky, he'll fire her.

Marlis drives to Natoli's Restaurant on The Promontory, the sheer granite cliff that gives the town its name. Two hundred feet below, icebergs the size of Volkswagens revolve in the swirling current of the river. A cloud drifts across the face of the sun and a sudden gust of wind pushes her forcefully toward the edge. She steps back with a small gasp and goes inside.

5

A Stranger at the Door

A knock on the front door of Lovelace House comes at one o'clock in the afternoon. Jennie peeks around the edge of the lace curtain that covers the glass oval in the door. A slender man about her age stands on the veranda. He wears jeans, a sheepskin jacket, a cowboy hat and well-traveled boots. Two salt-and-pepper braids fall over his shoulders, Willie Nelson-style.

'Oh, what now?' Miss Jennie is still dressed in her blue chenille robe and matching slippers. She woke in an ornery mood, as she often does in winter's endless imprisonment. She opens the door two inches. 'Talk fast,' she says. 'I'm losing heat.'

'I'm from Texas, ma'am,' he drawls. 'Talking fast is not in my genetic code. I'm Tex Roper, and — '

'No one's name is Tex Roper,' she says.

'Percy Theodore didn't draw the rodeo crowds the way Tex used to. The Roper part is real.'

'Well, Mr. Roper, either you're very late for the last rodeo, or very early for the next.'

'A little of both, I guess.'

'I'm Jennie Lovelace. Now that we're introduced, let's make this quick. If you're looking for money, you've come to the wrong house. If you're hungry, I'll make you a sandwich, but you'll have to take it with you.'

'I brought you something. It's in my car.'

'I'm not in a purchasing mood, Mr. Roper.'

'If you don't want it, I'll haul it off. You stay here and keep warm. I'll just be a minute.'

'Well, don't dawdle. My gas meter is clicking like a metronome.'

Tex walks beneath the oak trees to his car. Jennie notices a slight limp, a reminder that most cowboys end their careers pretty busted up. He lifts something of considerable weight from the trunk. When she sees it, she gives a whoop of delight, throws the door open and scurries across the veranda.

'Mr. Holzheimer! Where have you — ?' She clears three slippery steps, but number four gets her and she hits the ground with spine-jolting force. Tex drops the gnome in the snow bank and rushes to her side.

'Are you hurt?' he says, kneeling beside her. 'Is anything broken?'

'It's my ankle. And I felt my tailbone snap. Or did I hear it? I can't be sure.'

'Don't move.' He stands up, pulls out his cell phone, and dials 911. 'An elderly woman has taken a tumble on the ice. We need the first responders immediately.'

An elderly woman? He'd got nerve! 'Tell them no sirens,' she says. 'No need to put on a dog-and-pony-show for the neighbors.'

'Yes, that's Lovelace House on Euclid. She's likely broken a bone or two.' The operator tries to keep him on the line but he clicks off. 'Take my hand and I'll help you up. Very slowly now.'

She rises on her good foot, his arm around her waist, firmly supporting her ascent. 'I'll never make it up those damned steps,' she says.

He sweeps her into his arms before she can protest, carries her into the house, and shoves the door closed with his foot. 'Which way to the bedroom?'

'First door on the right.'

He settles her carefully on the bed and removes her right slipper. The ankle is swollen and blue. She tries to be brave, but gives a little mouse squeak of pain. Tex finds the kitchen, returns with a zipper baggy of ice, wraps it in his bandanna, and puts it on her ankle.

The front door opens and Rosalie enters the hall. She stops and looks into the bedroom. 'What's happened, Miss Jennie?'

'I had a slip on the ice. Mr. Roper, this is Rosalie, one of my tenants.'

'Pleased to meet you, young lady.'

'Can I do something to help?'

'I don't think so,' he says.

'The medics are on their way,' says Jennie. 'I'm sure I'll be fine.'

After Rosalie goes upstairs, Jennie asks Tex if he would bring in Mr. Holzheimer. Within a minute the gnome is brushed free of snow and sitting in the corner of her room.

'From now on he stays inside. He's too great a temptation for the neighborhood hooligans.' She puts on her bifocals and looks Tex up and down. 'I suppose you've come for the reward.'

'What reward?'

'The $25, of course.'

'I wouldn't know about that, ma'am.'

'Where did you find him?'

'In the field across the road. His hat was peeking above the snow. That was three or four days ago.'

'You *were* waiting for the reward.'

'I was not!'

She tries to roll onto an elbow, but winces with pain and collapses back on the pillow.

'When I found him he'd lost his hatchet. I wanted to repair it before I brought him back. I see him in your yard every time I go down No Name Road to the trailer park.'

'You know someone who lives in that mud hole?'

He pauses. 'I live there.' An awkward silence stretches between them, finally broken by the sound of approaching sirens. The first responders tramp up the veranda steps.

'Good day, Miss Lovelace,' says Tex, touching the brim of his hat. 'I leave you in good hands.'

She tries to come up with a redeeming word, but for once she's at a loss.

★ ★ ★

When I return to the site of the homicide, Sheriff Brooker's patrol car and the forensic van are on site. As I get out of the car, a 1950s pickup truck pulls to the shoulder on the far side of the road. A pretty young woman and a little boy run across the highway hand in hand. An elderly man remains in the truck.

'Nancy, thank god!'

'Uncle Nicky!' shrieks the boy, jumping into his arms. Nick holds them both in his embrace.

'I've never been happier to see anyone in my life,' he says.

'When you didn't show, I knew it had to be that bald tire. Daddy brought chains, and I've got a chicken roasting back at the house.'

I walk up to Nick. 'You dropped this,' I say, handing him his phone.

'Thank you, ma'am. Thank you for everything. I really mean that.'

'A night in the cold can be a life-altering experience.'

'So can a few other things.'

I duck beneath the crime-scene tape and cross the ditch. Everyone is huddled around the death tree trying to decide how to extricate the man in the least destructive manner. There are a few nods and hellos as I join the circle. Frack walks over and stands by my side as the forensic photographer finishes his shoot.

'His arms are frozen around the damn tree,' says Sheriff Ernie Brooker, a middle-aged, matter-of-fact man who does double duty as coroner. He takes a key and unlocks The Iceman's cuffs.

'Don't force his arms,' says Paula. 'I

want him on the autopsy table in one piece.'

'Anyone got a better idea?' says Brooker.

'I have,' I say. 'We need to talk to the man with the truck before he drives off.'

'That guy with the firewood?' says Paula.

'He's a skilled lumberjack. How about we at least get his take on the situation?'

'Okay,' says Brooker. 'Can't hurt.'

'I'll get him,' offers Frack.

In five minutes Frack returns with Nick. He's carrying a chainsaw that could cut a barn in half. 'Nick discovered the body, which gives us a timeline to work with,' I say. 'Otherwise the Iceman might have gone unnoticed for months.'

'Here's our problem,' says the sheriff to Nick. 'We need our victim out of here in one piece.'

'You got any sentiments regarding the tree?' asks Vanderhoot.

'You seen one, you seen 'em all.'

Nick circuits the tree. He's had time for the morning's initial shock to wear off. This time he avoids a stare-down with those unblinking blue eyes. 'Everyone stand back,' he says. We give him all the room he needs. He ties his hair back with a thong. 'I knew a man caught his hair in the chain. Looked like he'd been scalped by Comanches. Then there was this guy up Eagle River way . . . '

'With all due respect,' says Sheriff Brooker, 'if I want a horror story, I'll read my nephew's rap sheet.' A round of nervous laughter eases the tension in the air. Nick adjusts his noise protectors.

The saw roars to life and wood chips fly like bullets. We back off several more steps and cover our ears. The first cut removes the small branch the handcuffs are looped over. He tosses the limb aside. The Iceman's arms remain raised in supplication to a god who can't find his way through the north woods. Next he makes a skillful notch in the tree above the wrists and gives the branch a push. There's a sharp crack and it lands exactly where he said it would.

'One more cut should do it. I need volunteers to keep the fellow upright just in case.' Frack and one of the forensic men volunteer. Nick makes a cut below the wrists that goes all the way through the tree and stops millimeters short of The Iceman's brown plaid coat. The saw chokes to a stop but my ears will ring for another fifteen minutes. Nick removes his noise protectors and forensics takes over. They ease The Iceman away from the lower portion of trunk. There's a crisp tearing sound as his frozen coat pulls away from the bark.

'That's it,' says Nick. 'He's all yours.' Sheriff Brooker tries to slip him a hundred-dollar bill. With a shake of the head, Nick waves it away and walks back to the road.

'Danner, I'm appointing you lead on the case,' says the sheriff. 'Partner with Frack. Mike can man the station and guard the donuts.' That gets a snicker or two. 'You work your end, while Paula and I work ours.'

'Yes, sir,' I say.

'Get this man to the van,' says Brooker. 'We can't crunch him into a body bag, so we'll carry him on a blanket. It's my first experience with a human totem pole.'

Paula and her team stay behind to process the scene. 'If we find I.D. on the body, we'll let you know,' she tells me. 'I can't do much more until he thaws out. Call me around noon tomorrow. I should know something by then.'

'You got it,' I say.

Nick's truck is gone when Frack and I cross the ditch. Across the road a van is idling on the shoulder, the driver gawking at the crime tape. When he sees us the truck jumps forward, snow and gravel spraying from beneath the tires.

'That was weird,' I say, as we climb into the car.

'People see crime tape, they want to know what's going on.'

'That's funny. I'd like to know what's going on too.'

★   ★   ★

The pressure in Larry's head threatens to rip apart the tectonic plates of his skull. He took a wrong turn an hour back and has no idea where he is. He never again wants to slow for an Amish buggy or eat a cheese curd or hear the words *Yeah, you betcha*. He wants to breathe car exhaust and factory smoke and blend in with the other nameless boogeymen who hide in the shadows of big cities.

He's driving on fumes, the engine stuttering, when he pulls into a rural gas station/convenience store shortly after dark. From a rack outside the door, a facsimile of his face stares at him from the front page of the *Post Crescent* — black mole and all. The clerk, a grizzled old cuss, squints at him through the glass door and reaches for the phone. Larry jumps back in the car and takes off.

He's gone 100 yards when a cop car pulls behind him. He stomps the gas pedal and shoots over the pavement. The gas gauge hits empty. The power brakes freeze. The steering locks. At 65 miles an hour, he hydroplanes over black ice, bounces across the roadside ditch, and chops off a telephone pole three feet above the ground. The pole lands squarely atop the Lincoln. Electricity goes out as far as the eye can see. People jump from their easy chairs, throw coats over their pajamas, and race to the scene. It takes the Jaws of Life two hours to extract the dead man from the crushed car.

'Too bad about the Lincoln,' says Deputy Swenson.

'Yeah, too bad,' says Deputy Nordyke. 'Must have cost a pretty penny.'

'Yeah, you betcha, a pretty penny. The driver was sure a skittish fellow,' says Swenson. 'I only wanted to tell him his seat belt was dragging on the ground.'

'Too late now. Grab the briefcase there. We'll open it back at the station. Maybe he was a jewelry salesman, this guy.'

'He was a fancyman of some kind, all right.'

'Did you see those Italian leather shoes?'

'No good for cleaning up after the cows.'

'You can say that again. One thing's for sure, he's not from around here.'

★ ★ ★

The house is quiet. Marlis passes Miss Jennie's closed bedroom door and treads quietly up the stairs. Rosalie is tossing and mumbling in her sleep. Marlis touches the girl's burning forehead and mixes a fizzy fever remedy in a glass of water. She helps Rosalie sit up just long enough to drink it and collapse back on the pillow.

'There, that should bring the fever down.'

Rosalie grabs her sleeve. 'He's hiding under the bridge. He tore my dress.'

'It's only a nightmare,' says Marlis, pushing a damp lock of hair away from the girl's face. 'You're perfectly safe now.' But even as she says it, she senses that the torn dress is more memory than nightmare.

★ ★ ★

After filling Big Mike in on what we now label The Iceman Case, he leaves to pick up the triplets, and Frack and I work late at the computer. There's still a BOLO out across the upper midwest for David Dorne Coburn, 47 years old, 6 ft., black hair, brown eyes, last seen wearing a green plaid coat and matching cap.

'Coburn can't be The Iceman,' says Frack. 'He doesn't match the physical description, and none of the tow companies have picked up an Elan van. Unless someone reports him missing, there's not much more we can do unless Paula finds I.D. on him.'

Bone weary, we lock up and head for the car. 'How about a nice steamy shower?' says Frack as we drive the few blocks toward home. 'I'll even shampoo your hair.'

'Sounds heavenly, as long as I don't have to jump in a snowbank afterward.'

'That's for the Swedes. A hardy bunch, those Swedes. I'm thinking warm brandy and German chocolate cake.'

'Now you're talking my language.'

★   ★   ★

Deputies Swenson and Nordyke set the briefcase on a table in the interrogation room of the small Dane Rock Sheriff's Station. Swenson picks off a key taped to the underside. 'Here, you do the honors.'

'What if there's a bomb inside?'

'It would have gone off when he hit the pole. I'm thinking jewelry or drugs.'

Nordyke twists the key in the lock and opens the case. 'Let's see. We've got duct tape, zip ties, handcuffs and — handcuffs?'

'By golly, Cal. This is a murder kit. Maybe he's the fellow in the newspaper. Did you see a black mole on his face when they pulled him from the wreck?'

'There was no face. He left it on the dashboard.'

6

Chilling Revelations

Rosalie's fever is gone in the morning. Weak and listless, she comes downstairs in sweats and pokes her head into Miss Jennie's bedroom.'

'Come in, dear.'

'What did they say at the hospital?'

'I have a broken tailbone, but the doctor calls it a fractured coccyx so he can charge more money,' she says.

'What about the ankle?'

'It's a bad sprain. I'll be off my feet for a while. Mrs. Berry from church picked me up from the hospital and the nurse sent me home with a walker. It has a seat so I can push myself around with one foot.'

'Can I fix you something?'

'Coffee and a bowl of Cheerios would be nice.'

'Have you seen Sylvia?'

'She picked up some clothes. She looks like a girl in love, if you ask me.'

After Miss Jennie is finished eating, Rosalie rinses the bowl and rearranges her pillows. 'Will you do something for me?' Jennie says. 'I was rude to Mr. Roper yesterday. I'll read you my apology, and you tell me what you think.'

'Okay.'

'If it weren't for him, I never would have gotten Mr. Holzheimer back.' She holds a piece of blue stationery under the lamp. 'Dear Mr. Roper — '

'Too formal.'

Jennie makes the correction. 'Dear Tex.'

'Much better.'

'Okay, here we go. Dear Tex: It was kind of you to return Mr. Holzheimer and help me when I fell. Please accept my apology for yesterday's rudeness. I'd be honored if you'd join me for tea this afternoon at three o'clock. Sincerely, Your Neighbor, Jennie Lovelace.'

'Perfect,' says Rosalie. 'Let me deliver it.'

'Thank you, dear. That would be lovely.' Jennie folds the note and puts it inside a matching envelope. 'He lives in the trailer park.'

'What space number?'

'You'll have to ask. Get a reply if you can. He might not want anything to do with me. Look at me, Rosalie. You're very pale. You're not coming down with something, are you?'

'I'm just tired. I'm going to read in my room when I get back.'

*   *   *

Eighteen-year-old Billy Breen turns off the highway onto Burnt Barn Road, a long driveway through the woods to an abandoned farm and a heap of charred wood that used to be the barn. His muscle-truck with its gargantuan tires is one of the few vehicles that can drive in and out of deep snow without getting stuck. He stops just this side of a rusted gate, about to illegally dump his household trash, when he sees a van lodged against a tree twenty feet down the bank, all but one letter of the signage covered in snow. He yells a 'Hello down there' but receives no reply. He's curious, but not so curious that he wants to trudge down the bank and get his pants legs wet. He pulls out his cell phone and makes an anonymous call to the station in Abundance, then gets back on the highway. Burnt Barn Road isn't the only place he can dump his trash.

* * *

We park along the highway and walk down the road in the tire tracks left by the anonymous caller. My nose is numb, my lungs aching with every breath. 'This better not be a crank call,' I say, my teeth chattering.

'Better not be,' Frack echoed.

'Ever think of moving to Florida?'

'They have hurricanes, Robely.'

'Los Angeles?'

'Earthquakes.'

'I don't care,' I say. 'I want to live in a place where I can get an all-over tan in January.'

'When do we leave?'

'Last fall would have been perfect,' I

say through chattering teeth.

After fifteen minutes, we reach the gate and look into the ravine. The van leans away from us against a tree halfway down the slope.

'There it is, just like he said. Let's do it,' says Frack.

We jump over the edge and wade to the van through waist-deep snow. 'The license plate matches the missing van,' says Frack. The back doors are open, the interior blown with snow. The garment racks are empty, but for one trampled fur left on the floor.

'Cleaned out,' I say. 'How far is this from the murder tree?'

'I don't know. Maybe a hundred yards. Someone else can walk it off.' Working against gravity, Frack pulls the driver's door up and open, and I drop inside beneath the steering wheel.

'The keys are in the ignition,' I say. 'Not that it's going anywhere.'

I bag whatever flotsam and jetsam I find scattered around the interior — a bag of potato chips, a paper coffee cup, a singed but unsmoked cigarette. There are crumpled Camels packs, a receipt, stray pennies and a few bottle caps. Next, I search the glove box. I find the truck registration and a two-year-old traffic ticket with Coburn's name on it. I toss those, along with a hard pack of Marlboros — one cigarette missing — into the bag. Wind whistles through the cab, the cold chilling the marrow of my bones.

'Come on,' says Frack. 'Pass me the bag.' I hand it over. He grabs the ruined garment from the back of the truck, slams the doors shut and pulls me up the bank to the road.

★   ★   ★

After lunch, Marlis parks in the garage at Bratton's. A big white dog with a head the size of a boxcar skids around the corner of the building, dragging a heavy chain. The dog's growl is cut short when he flips at the end of the chain two feet away from where she stands. She's frozen against the car door, her knees buckling, the briefcase dropping from her hand. It opens on impact and Ruth's diary slides onto the ground.

Bull materializes from the shadows, laughing like it's all a big joke. He bunts the dog in the chest with his knee and bends over to pick up the diary. He flips casually through the pages.

'Women,' he says with disgust. Not realizing what he's holding, he tosses it in the briefcase and snaps it shut. The dog lowers his head, menacing and wild-eyed. His ears are clipped flush to the skull, his face and body grilled with scars from the dog-fighting ring. Marlis snatches her briefcase from Bull's hand.

'I see you've met Jack,' he says, jovially. 'It's short for Jack the Ripper. Now *that's* a guard dog.'

'Get out of my face,' says Marlis, shoving him forcefully aside and giving the dog a wide berth. She strides across the yard and enters her office. When she hears Bratton jogging after her, she locks the door and leans trembling against it. She takes two long draws from her inhaler.

He tries the knob. 'Come on, can't you

take a joke?' He pounds his fist against the door. She walks across the room, hands supporting her weight on the desktop. She looks in the mirror. Her face is white, tears swimming in her blue eyes. Bull kicks the door a couple times and gives up.

She stands perfectly still until she hears him enter his cave. As his door opens, a bright blade of light slices across the mirror. The door closes and the light is gone. Now she understands Benny's warning. Bratton can observe her through a two-way mirror. The light she'd seen in the glass had been coming from the next room, from a video recorder or a cigar. She scrambles to remember what she'd said on the phone that night but can't focus.

Marlis rushes out the door and starts across the yard. Bull's door flies open. He's right behind her, grabbing her arm, pulling her to a stop. 'Where do you think you're going?'

'Let go of my arm.'

He looks around. 'Where's my dog?'

She jerks her arm free. 'With Dr.

111

Alderman at the Promontory Veterinary Clinic.'

'What the hell?'

Benny Goddard is suddenly at her side. 'What's going on?' he says.

'We're just having a little talk — aren't we, Miss Underhill?'

'I'm going home,' she says. 'I'm not feeling well.'

'What about the IRS?'

'You should have thought about that a long time ago.'

He holds out his hand, his face a giant red radish. 'Give me my gate key.'

She hands over the original and almost tells him where he can insert it. He doesn't demand her office key. He doesn't tell her she's fired. She finds it all very odd.

'I'll walk you to your car,' says Benny. When they get closer to the dog, he says, 'Give me your car keys and wait here.' He walks around the end of Jack's chain. The dog goes ballistic, choking himself as he strains against his collar. Benny eases the car out of the garage. He climbs out and holds the door open for her.

'Thank you, Benny.' Marlis gets in and he closes the door. A half mile down the road, hands shaking, she pulls over and calls the veterinary hospital.

'This is Vickie. How may I help you?'

'Hello, Vickie. This is Marlis Underhill checking on Rommel.'

'Dr. Alderman is out right now, but Rommel is resting peacefully. We need to keep him another day or two. He has a bad sprain and five cracked ribs, but given a little T.L.C. he'll recover nicely.'

'Can I visit him?'

'He won't understand when you leave without him.'

'I hadn't thought of that. I'll check in again tomorrow. If you get a call from a Mr. Bratton . . . '

'I know all about it. We won't release the dog to anyone but you.'

★　★　★

Sylvia and Kent are sleeping when the phone rings. It's the kind of morning where no one wants to crawl out from their warm cocoon. 'It better not be somebody selling something,' she says. She checks the caller I.D. and her expression brightens. 'It's Cousin Luisa.'

'Maybe she's found a husband,' says Kent in his raspy morning voice.

She presses the talk button. 'Luisa, what a nice surprise. Is everything all right?'

'Yes and no. I've had another gallstone attack. If they were diamonds I'd be rich, but they look like sharp glass snowflakes under the scanner.'

'Ouch!'

'I'll be closing the inn for a few days after surgery. I asked Mother to come, but she doesn't want to break up her bridge foursome. She won't drive in the snow, and if I dare mention flying, she says, 'Have you forgotten Nine-Eleven? Are you really that eager to come into your inheritance?' What inheritance? She's leaving me a set of old dishes and her golf trophies.'

'And I thought I was getting the trophies.'

They burst into laughter like they did when they were kids.

'Would you like to keep me company for a few days? The fridge is stocked, and we'll have all 20,000 square feet to ourselves.'

'Like in *The Shining*? Snow on the roof. Jack Nicholson chasing us with a hatchet.'

'I have good locks on the doors.'

'Actually, it sounds heavenly, but I'm working at the Bar and Grill, and — '

'I'll get Shorty's wife to fill in,' says Kent, rolling out of bed. 'I'm going downstairs to make coffee.'

'I heard that,' says Luisa. 'You're in bed with a man!'

'I'm in bed with *the* man. His name is Kent Longtree.'

'Am I invited to the wedding?'

'No one's invited to the wedding. It's going to be a quick trip to the justice of the peace.'

'You're in a family way.'

'I'm not! How about you visit us when the weather's nice?'

'You mean you're moving to the Virgin Islands?'

'Come on, Luisa,' Sylvia laughs. 'We

always have a window of lovely weather in July — green fields, lakes full of fish, wildflowers everywhere. You have harsher weather in Manitowish Waters.'

'Maybe so, but we have Little Bohemia Lodge, the site of the FBI/Dillinger shootout of 1934. The bullet holes are still in the walls. Try to beat that.'

'You fail to mention that the FBI shot three innocent people and the Dillinger Gang made a clean getaway.'

'A minor detail.'

'I'll do you one better. Ninety-year-old Jasper Olson leads the Fourth of July parade riding his Holstein cow and carrying the American flag.'

Luisa roars with laughter. 'That I must see.'

'I'm holding you to that. Now fill me in on what I need to know.'

'The doctor is waiting for an opening in the surgery schedule, so it'll be short notice. Can you handle that?'

'I don't see why not.'

'You're an angel. How is Rosalie? I haven't heard from her in a while.'

Sylvia hears Kent coming back up the

stairs. 'We'll talk about it when I see you.'

'Are you implying that Rosie is still Rosie?'

'A rose is a rose is a rose.'

'Didn't Shakespeare say that?'

'It was Gertrude Stein.'

That sends Luisa into stitches of laughter.

★　★　★

Deputies Don Swenson and Cal Nordyke know this will probably be the most infamous incident they will ever be associated with. There is no doubt that the deceased is the Traveling Butcher; but what is his true identity? Where is he from?

Until now, Dane Rock's biggest crime spree was the missing box of Mars Bars from the convenience store. Swenson and Nordyke diligently followed the candy wrapper clues to the door of a ten-year-old truant, Cody Matson. The weekly newspaper labeled it 'The Hansel and Gretel Heist,' and everyone got a big kick out of it.

Now they're involved in a real grown-up mystery.

The only clues to the dead man's identity are the police rendering and the fingerprints from the car. His wallet contains $300, but no driver's license, personal information, or family photos. His fingerprints have been run through the database, which came up with no matches. It's unlikely that he'd ever been in the military, held a civil service job or been convicted of a crime. The Lincoln had been stolen in Des Moines, the gun was from a shop in Cincinnati, and the hat was from a haberdashery in Chicago. The man without a face would be buried without a name.

★   ★   ★

Miss Jennie and Tex Roper sit in front of the crackling fireplace, she in her walker and he in a comfortable armchair, the small table between them set with tea and cookies. Jennie is in her blue robe, Tex fit to kill in polished cowboy boots and red snap-button shirt.

'I see Mr. Holzheimer has found a place on the hearth,' says Tex.

'I don't trust him the way I used to. I never noticed that wicked little spark in his eye until he came inside.'

Tex smiles. 'Hard to tell what he's capable of.'

'At least he won't be walking away again,' she says, stirring her tea. She settles back and studies Tex's face. 'Why Abundance?' she asks. 'You must have travelled to far more interesting places on the rodeo circuit.'

'It's the last place I got bucked off. It's a young man's game and I stayed at it too long. The owner of the trailer park, a big fan of mine, took me in while I recuperated from a few busted bones. He was getting too old to keep the place up, and then a couple months ago his wife was diagnosed with Alzheimer's. I made him a cash offer. He accepted and they moved to Miami.'

'A cash offer? We don't see many of those around here.'

'I've never been hitched and I have no drinking or gambling habits, so for years I squirreled my money away. When I was young, I thought I'd buy me a spread back in Texas, but I waited too long. My parents are gone and my extended family is scattered, so there's no one to go back to.'

'So you bought . . . '

'That mud hole? Yes. It *is* a mud hole, but there are a lot of nice folks living there, even if they don't have two cents to rub together.'

'I regret saying what I did yesterday. I think you know that.'

'It's forgotten. As soon as the weather warms up, I'm hauling away the trash, making repairs, and spiffing up the joint. I'm going to pave No Name Road and give it a real name with some dignity. Any ideas?'

Jennie refills his tea cup and gives the matter some thought. 'How about New Hope Road?'

'New Hope Road. Yes, I like that.'

Rosalie pops her head around the door frame with a book in her hand. 'Miss Jennie?'

'What is it, dear?'

'I'm sorry to interrupt, but the chimney's leaking smoke again. You can smell it real strong on the second-floor landing.'

'I'll have the handyman look into it when he comes to fix the window. I'm sure all it needs is a good clean.'

Rosalie retrieves the newspaper from the porch and goes back upstairs, closing the attic door to keep out the smell.

'You want me to check out the chimney?' says Tex.

'I didn't invite you here to work on the house.' She nibbles delicately on her cookie. 'The doctor says I should be good as new by the end of May. My garden shed is full of seeds and cuttings. I could help brighten up the park with some roses and snapdragons.'

'The place could sure use some cheering up.'

'It's settled then,' she says, 'provided those runny-nosed ragamuffins don't drive me off. We don't get along, you know.'

'Then stop throwing snowballs at them when they cross your lawn. Bring them some of these cookies. It'll work wonders.'

After a pleasant hour of conversation, Tex thanks Jennie for a lovely afternoon and makes his exit.

Upstairs, Rosalie unfolds the newspaper. The front page is devoted to the wreckage left by the storm: collapsed porches, crumpled cars, a cow frozen against a fence, roofs with spines crushed by fallen trees. Even The Iceman Murder Case is relegated to page two.

She turns the page and a headline jumps out at her: 'Traveling Butcher Dies in One-car Crash.' The police sketch is of Larry, complete with dark glasses and black mole. She reads the article, her hands turning cold.

Why did he let her live? Why isn't her body in a cornfield and her head in a creek bed like the others? She finishes off a bottle of brandy. It takes more and more alcohol to wash away her disappointments and oblique longings.

Downstairs in the parlor, Miss Jennie tosses a handful of pinecones into the fire. As she leans back in her walker, a chunk of broken brick tumbles down the chimney onto the grate.

'Where in the world did that come from?' she says.

★   ★   ★

Marlis can't wait to read the diary. She stops at a country café and orders coffee. Beyond the window, snowflakes turn to rain, and a sparkling crust ices over the snowbanks. She arranges the contents of Ruth's purse on the tabletop: the diary, an address book, a small bag of peanuts, a black matchbook from Vittoni's Bar in Appleton. She opens the diary and begins reading.

Argued with Violet. She's got a ramrod up her spine. Doesn't want Phyllis coming around anymore.

Investigation Discovery tonight. Dateline — 48 Hours — Joe Kenda, Homicide Hunter.

Poor Al. Back in the hospital. Third time in as many weeks.

Al back home. Feeling slightly better. Bull and Claudine pay him a visit.

Al back in hospital.

Bull purchasing wildly. The Paxtons are hiring a lawyer to examine the company books.

Christmas night. Party at Paxton's. Everyone from the storage facility is there. Al is confined to a wheelchair. He's a yellow-eyed skeleton who can't remember my name. He whispers something in my ear. I see Bull watching us. Must tell Julie. I corner her but Bull follows us into the den so we can't talk in private. He has two drinks in hand and says one is for Al. He's not a skilled liar.

'I'll find him,' says Claudine, taking one of the flutes from his hand and waltzing out of the room. Julie is called out of the room by a guest. My opportunity to speak with her passes. Al dies that night. I never talk with Julie again.

Tonight at ten. Homicide Hunter.

The next day she makes her final entry.

The answer is in the crystals.

124

Marlis reads it again. What crystals? The answer to what? She's writing in secret code.

Violet Chambers is listed in Ruth's address book. Same last name. They have to be related. Marlis calls the number and the answering machine picks up: 'Violet here. I can't come to the phone. If you're Ruth, please come home. If you've seen Ruth or her car, leave your number and I'll return your call.'

Marlis hangs up without leaving a message. She finds Phyllis McCoy's phone number on Ruth's emergency contact card. After a moment's indecision, she taps in her number.

7

A Clue

Paula waves Frack and me into the autopsy room. It's frigid and smells of toxic chemicals and unpleasant body fluids. This is one instance when a deep breath does not ward off an upsurge of nausea.

'Anything new?' says Paula, turning from the autopsy table.

'Did you hear about the missing van out of Minnesota?' I ask.

'I saw it in the newspaper. Why?'

'We've just come from Burnt Barn Road. It's over the bank, not far from where our victim was found. It's been ransacked.'

'So The Iceman is the missing driver?'

'The BOLO gives the driver's name as David Dorne Coburn. Age 47. Black hair. Brown eyes.'

Paula gives me a puzzled look. 'Our

man is blond and blue-eyed. He can't be Coburn.'

'That's right, but I think the two are connected . . . maybe. Coburn has yet to surface. One trashed coat was left behind in the van. We brought in what evidence we found.'

'The sheriff will be down in a few minutes and we'll all have a look.' She motions us to the autopsy table. The Iceman lies on the cold aluminum surface, his face covered with a towel, his body draped in a sheet. Above the table is a scale, to the side a stainless steel tray of instruments. 'There's no need to uncover the face,' says Paula, pulling down the sheet and leaving the towel in place. 'He's every bit as handsome as he was yesterday.'

'Paula, for heaven's sake!'

'Sorry, Robely,' she says, suppressing a smile. She turns to the body. 'I found no blood, no bullet holes, and no stab wounds.'

'So he's not really dead?' says Frack. 'What a relief.'

'You're as bad as she is,' I say. 'Paula,

would you please cut to the chase.'

'Okay. Cause of death: exposure. Manner of death: homicide. No surprises there.'

'If one person heard his cries, we wouldn't be here,' I say.

'The Iceman's larynx was badly crushed. He couldn't call for help. He received a single blow to the throat from something like a cane or a pipe. He was then tethered to the tree, where the elements finished him off. You can clearly see the pattern of bruising.' She lifts the towel to expose the throat. 'We're dealing with a sadistic psychopath, someone to whom violence is as natural as breathing. An estimated time of death will have to be determined by means other than autopsy. There you have it.'

Sheriff Brooker walks in. We talk briefly, and Paula pulls the sheet back over the corpse. As we walk down the hall to the conference room, I bring the sheriff up to speed. We take chairs around the table and Frack hangs the ruined coat over the back of a chair. I spread the contents of the evidence bag on the surface in front of us.

'It looks like the kind of litter you'd find in a ditch,' says Brooker.

'Someone was a bad housekeeper,' I say. 'We know from the snow covering the body that the homicide took place before the blizzard. The only footprints leading to the tree were those of Mr. Vanderhoot, who discovered the body, and the only tire tracks leading to the van were from the truck of the anonymous man who called in its location.'

'And?' says Brooker.

'I think our best evidence in determining the timeline is a receipt from the Stop and Go where Tammy Oxenburg works.' Tammy being the wife of Big Mike. 'The driver purchased a bag of potato chips, a cup of coffee, and a Marlboro hard pack at 7:05 p.m. The chips remain unopened, and the Marlboro had been lit but not smoked.'

'Is that significant?' says Paula.

'It means he was interrupted. At seven bucks a pack, no one lights a cigarette without the intention of smoking it. I'll talk to Tammy; she might remember something.'

'But the driver who's missing is not the guy who was cuffed to the tree,' says Brooker.

'It's possible The Iceman hijacked the van sometime after Coburn made his Wausau delivery.'

'Or Coburn picked up a hitchhiker,' says Paula.

'What about Coburn?' says Brooker. 'He could be out there in the woods.'

'I was able to roll The Iceman's fingerprints,' says Paula. 'I'll run them through the database and see what we come up with.'

'Good place to start,' says Brooker.

'There were six crumpled packs of Camel Straights in the van,' I say. 'That suggests Coburn, being the long-term driver, was the Camel smoker, and The Iceman, who had been in the truck a shorter period of time, smoked Marlboros.'

'What was he doing on Burnt Barn Road? It doesn't go anywhere,' Brooker says.

'Only the regular driver would have

known that. I think The Iceman pulled off the highway for a smoke and a snack. He didn't get his smoke and he didn't get his snack.'

'All this hoopla for a bunch of damn coats?' says the sheriff.

'Special coats,' I say. 'I did some Googling. Did you know Wisconsin harvests one million fox pelts annually? We lead the nation — a dubious distinction at best.'

'One million!' says Paula with a shiver.

'The most prized are from the silver fox. They're bred in captivity because the color is a mutation that seldom exists in the wild. The prices of the coats vary widely depending on the market, the style, and the quality of the pelts. I found one short jacket on the internet for $1,200. A long, high-end coat was going for $6,500. Elan Fashion Furs is known in the industry as a jobber, the last link in the chain of custody from raw pelt to the furrier's showroom.'

'You've certainly done your homework,' says Brooker.

'She always does her homework,' says

Paula, giving me a wry grin.

'While we're on the subject,' I say, 'fur farming is a brutal operation. It's been banned in the United Kingdom and should be banned everywhere. Check it out if you have the stomach for it.'

'Six thousand five hundred dollars!' says Brooker. 'Anyone around here with that kind of money would buy a hunting cabin or a breeding bull.'

'To get good money they'd need a fence in the big city,' says Frack. 'Because they're hot, they'd go for pennies on the dollar, but even at a quarter of their value they'd be worth a bundle. There should be thirty-nine of the original fifty out there. Ten were delivered in Wausau. One was ruined in the heist.'

'I can't remember the last time I saw a woman in a luxury fur,' I say. 'Wisconsin is a dress-down state.'

'I can,' says Paula. 'Last night. But it wasn't a woman.'

Every antenna in the room quivers. 'What do you mean?' I ask.

'Around midnight I picked up a jumper, the second in six months at the old Franklin Hotel just beyond the Promontory city limits. The place is depressing with a capital D. The elevator goes back to the Coolidge Administration, which explains why it doesn't go up and down anymore.'

'Are you sure it wasn't a fake?'

'Positive. There's this big guy always hangs out in the entry — six feet tall, red plume in a broad yellow hat. He has a disproportionate number of lady friends in mini-skirts and platform shoes. He always wears a raccoon coat *à la* the 1920s, but last night he was fit to kill in a new fur that swept the toes of his elevator boots. It didn't seem relevant to our case at the time.'

* * *

'I saw you put that orange soda under your coat, Jimmy Gatlin,' says Tammy to the ten-year-old boy standing in front of the refrigerator case. 'Put it back. One more time and I call your parents, you little hoodlum.'

Jimmy puts it back and sets Twinkies

on the counter, but Tammy refuses to ring them up. 'Out!' she says.

Frack and I push through the door. 'I didn't think they'd get here this fast,' says Tammy with a wink. 'I hope you've brought your handcuffs, because . . . '

Jimmy shoots past us and Tammy bursts into laughter.

'Hi, Tammy. Got a minute?' I ask.

'Sure.'

'How are the triplets? Over their colds and back in preschool, I hope.'

'You mean the three little terrorists? I'm turning them over to Homeland Security.' She gives me a shrewd look. 'Why do I have the feeling this isn't a social call?'

I take the receipt we found in the van and show it to her. 'Ring any bells?' I ask.

'Looks like every receipt that goes out the door. Coffee. Cigarettes. Snacks. It's what people live on these days.'

'How about a white van? The signage on the door reads 'Elan Fashion Furs.' '

'That I remember. It had Minnesota plates.'

'That's right. How about the guy who

made the purchase? Remember him?'

'No, can't say as I do.'

'Did you see a second person in the van?'

'I had people stacked up at the register, but one thing I do remember. When a cop car pulled in, the van pulled out.'

'One of our cars?'

'No. It was city.'

'New London? Promontory?'

'I wish I could say. When the van pulled away, the cop car pulled out in the opposite direction, then circled back. I figured he was about to give a speeding ticket. The cop never came back this way. So what's going on?'

'We were hoping you could tell us.'

★   ★   ★

Shortly after dark, Frack drops me in front of the station while he goes on a fast-food run. I give Big Mike an update on our progress or lack thereof. Considering his bad ankle, he's relieved to be assigned to the station while Frack and I do the heavy lifting. Mike's already ordered take-out pizza and has to pick Tammy up at the store. By the time he limps to his car, I'm opening the Murder Book. As it grows, it will contain daily reports, interviews, autopsy results, photos, and the evaluation of evidence as it comes in.

I'm warming coffee of indeterminate age when the door opens and a preteen girl walks in. She's accompanied by a whiskery terrier and a blast of air that flutters the papers on my desk.

'How may I help you?' I ask.

'I'm Janet Hillerman. Troubles came home from the woods with a wallet. There's no money, but Mom says to turn it in.' She hands me a sticky dog-chewed piece of leather. Inside is a mangled driver's license belonging to David Dorne Coburn of Wausau, Wisconsin.

Frack walks in the door and sets a warm bag on the desk. At the smell of food, Janet, who's at least 10 lbs. underweight, almost faints.

'Where's Mike?' says Frack.

'He's taking pizza home.'

'What's up?' he asks.

I hand him the wallet. 'This young lady is Janet Hillerman. Her dog found it in the woods.'

'Looks like he tried to eat it,' he says.

'He likes to chew things,' says Janet. 'He ate my brother's rubber snake.'

Frack looks through the contents. 'It's Coburn's.'

'It is,' I say.

'Where do you live, Janet?' says Frack.

'On the street behind the grain elevators. I'd better go.'

Frack slips her a ten. 'Your reward,' he says. She thanks him. He puts our fast-food order on the desk and hands her the bag with Mike's order, which is always two of everything.

'Thank you so much,' she says. 'We don't get to the Bluebird very often.'

'How did you get here?'

'My bike.'

'Come on, I'll drive you home. We'll throw the bike in the back.'

As soon as they're gone, I call Paula. She picks up on the first ring, shouting into my ear. 'I ran the prints, Robely. They belong to a criminal named Harry Joe Madden.'

'Good job!'

'Madden's been busted for aggravated assault, armed robbery, DWI, and public drunkenness, all out of Wausau.'

'Now we're cooking. I've got one for you. A dog found Coburn's wallet in the woods. There's little doubt he was hijacked.'

'So was Madden,' she says. 'There's still a killer out there.'

'This couldn't get much weirder. But just because Coburn's wallet made it out of the city, doesn't mean he did.'

* * *

Bull explodes when he sees Hank Logan fooling with the lock on storage unit #20. He spins him around and belly-bumps him into the roll-up aluminum door. The concussion sounds like a train wreck, but the young man is country tough, surprised but unhurt.

'What the hell do you think you're doing?' says Hank.

'Where did you get that key?'

'Off the hook in the office. Isn't this the

unit we're auctioning off? I was going to inventory the contents.'

'Have you been inside?'

A brief pause, just long enough to come up with the right answer. 'Not yet. What's the big deal?'

Bull snatches the lock from Hank's hand and sinks it in the snowbank. He tosses the key on the roof of the building.

'Are you nuts?' says Hank.

'This is my brother's unit.' A vein pops in Bull's left eye, flooding the white with scarlet.

'Hey man, I think you're due for a rabies booster.' Hank shoulders past him and jumps in his pickup.

'From now on if I want something done, I'll tell you what and when,' he yells at his nephew's tail-lights. Burgess would have his head on a platter if any of his junk went missing.

★   ★   ★

Vittoni's is your typical urban pub, all oak and frosted glass. A woman in an orange jumpsuit and fluffy red-gold hair raises a finger. Marlis slides into the booth across from her. 'Thanks for agreeing to meet with me.'

'No problem,' says Phyllis.

The bartender walks over. 'What'll it be?'

'A Coke for me,' says Marlis.

'I'll have one more of these, Joe,' says Phyllis, her silver charm bracelet jingling against the side of her gimlet glass.

'You say you work for Bratton,' says Phyllis.

'Yes. I'm here because I'm concerned about Ruth Chambers. When did you see her last?'

'The night before she disappeared. It's been weeks now.'

'Has she been in touch with anyone since then?'

'If she had, it would have been me.' Joe sets their drinks in front of them and Marlis pays for the round. 'Had you known her long?' Phyllis asks.

'I never met her.' Phyllis looks at her with vague skepticism. 'I was hired after she left.' She slides the purse across the table to Phyllis, who looks stunned.

'That's Ruth's. Where did you find it?'

'In a filing cabinet at work. It seems intact — wallet, money, makeup.'

'Why call me?'

'You were on her emergency contact card, so I figured she trusts you.'

'Did you show this to Bull?'

'No. I doubt he knew it was there. I called Violet Chambers first but got the machine.'

'Vi is Ruth's older sister, a surgical nurse. When my relationship with Ruth went from friendship to something more deeply committed, I became persona non grata. Vi could no longer pretend not to notice Ruth's sexual proclivities.' She lights a cigarette. 'Are you shocked?'

'No. Are you disappointed?'

'You're quick. I like that.'

'I believe Ruth knew something about Bull Bratton, something he didn't want anyone to know.'

She gives Marlis a curious look. 'Are you a lawyer? Is there some hidden agenda here?'

'I'm a CPA. I crunch numbers. I'm only here because of the purse. I thought you should have it. She left a diary. You need to read it.'

'Have you?'

'Enough to know Ruth was concerned about something.'

'Did you find car keys?'

'No. Has anyone seen her car?'

Phyllis shakes her head.

'You must have reported her missing by now.'

'I went to the Promontory Police Department. They wouldn't let me file a missing persons report because I wasn't a relative.'

'Do you have to be?'

'I don't know,' Phyllis said. 'The desk sarge was about to hand me a form when Chief Bratton stared him down. Vi tried next. She had no more luck than I did. Chief Bratton said Ruth was seen only a few days ago at the Ho-Chunk Casino. That's a lie. Ruth is tight with money; won't even spring for a lotto ticket.'

'All the more reason she wouldn't leave her purse behind. The chief — is he related to Will?'

'Bull's older brother. Two apples from

the same twisted tree. What if I set up a brainstorming session with Vi and Albert's widow, Julie?'

'Will Vi meet with you?'

'Regarding Ruth's disappearance she will.'

'I have to go. I wish you luck.'

'Not so fast. I want you there. You're the only one of us with access to the storage yard. You could come in handy.'

Marlis writes her phone number on a napkin. 'Just tell me when and where. In the meantime, see what you make of the diary.'

★   ★   ★

Hank lies back in the big bed at Chateau du Lac. His head rests on his folded arm, a lock of hair drifting over one eye. Claudine runs her polished fingernails slowly over his hard six-pack, sending an electrifying ripple through his body. She's soft and perfumed and uninhibited. He's never known anyone quite like her.

'What would you do if Will walked in on us?' she says playfully.

'He won't. I punctured one of his tires. How did you end up getting hitched to that barbarian?' he says. 'It's like the mating of a gazelle and a hippopotamus.'

'He sleeps down the hall. I sleep with a Luger. It's my answer to birth control.'

'Bedtime and bullets. How cozy.'

She lights a cigarette, takes a slow drag, and puts it between his lips. 'How did you end up with Melinda?'

He pulls in smoke and blows it casually toward the ceiling. 'She was pregnant. It was a long time ago.'

'Your kid?'

'Who knows? We tied the knot. She miscarried. We got an annulment and she married the preacher's son.'

'You are so full of it,' she scoffs.

'It's true. She wanted to know what a real man was like before she chained herself to the church pew.'

'She should have asked me.'

'Do you think I've forgotten my question?'

'What question?' She rolls onto an elbow, her golden-blonde hair falling long and loose.

'The one about Bull. Why you married him. And don't tell me you needed a storage yard.'

'Does it matter?'

'It matters,' he says, with just the right edge to his voice.

'We belonged to the same flying club.'

'You flew a plane?'

'I did, but Daddy did most of the piloting. When my parents passed, I was very young. Will was a comforting presence, sort of a father figure. You know what they say — marry in haste, regret at leisure.'

'Your throat turns red when you lie.' The silence stretches between them. 'What does he have on you?'

'Why all the questions? Let's just say that if I have his back, he has mine.'

'That's a little vague, Claudine.'

'What if he wasn't around anymore? It would be just you and me.'

His cynical laughter isn't what she expects from a man. 'Bringing you breakfast on a silver tray?' he says. 'Walking your poodle along the lake? No thank you. I don't want anything from you that I don't already have; and if you don't want to give it, I'll get it elsewhere.'

'You are one hard man,' she says.

'I'm just not as stupid as you want me to be. I've seen *Double Indemnity*.'

'I spoke to Ruth Chambers's replacement,' she says, changing the subject.

'Miss Underhill?'

'Yes. What's she like?'

'Young. Smart.'

'Smart enough to get Will square with the IRS?'

'I'm sure she knows how to do her job.'

'That's good. I don't want his financial problems landing me on the evening news. Is she pretty?'

'What does it matter? She can do long division in her head.'

'Never mind. I'll ask her to the house and decide for myself.'

She takes the cigarette from his hand and sets it smoking in the ashtray.

'Okay,' she sighs. 'You know how I like it.'

★ ★ ★

It's well after dark when Jennie hears a car door close in front of the house. Chimes sound in the quiet hall.

'I'll get it,' calls Rosalie, coming from the kitchen. She looks through the window in the front door and sees a man in an expensive overcoat and leather gloves. At his side is a big dog wrapped in bandages. She opens the door.

'Good evening,' he says. 'Is Miss Underhill in?'

'I'm afraid she's not home yet.'

'I'm Mark Alderman, her veterinarian.'

'I didn't know she had one.'

He pats Rommel's head. 'She rescued this fellow from a bad situation. He's doing much better, so I thought I'd drop him off and save her the trip into Promontory.'

'Who is it?' snaps Miss Jennie. 'You're letting the heat out. Bring him in here and make sure he wipes his feet on the mat.'

He steps inside and sets a big bag of dog food in the entryway. Rosalie leads him to the bedroom door. 'This is Mr. Alderman, a friend of Marlis's,' she says.

'This is Miss Jennie Lovelace, our landlady.'

The moment Rommel sees the old lady, his ears prick up, his eyes brighten, and he wags his tail. Tears leap into Jennie's eyes.

'Woofie! Where have you been?'

Rommel forgets his injuries. He jumps up on the bed with a wince of pain and lies down beside her. Of course, he looks nothing like her long-lost spaniel, but she doesn't seem to notice. He licks her cheek. He nibbles her ear and makes her laugh, then rests his muzzle on her shoulder.

'Is she always a bit — confused?' whispers Mark.

'She lost a dog years ago and never got over it.'

'Shall I leave him?' he asks.

'Does it look like she's going to give him up?'

He shakes his head. 'I don't think so. He needs his follow-up visit in two weeks.'

'I'll tell Marlis.'

He hands Rosalie an envelope with

Marlis's name on the front. 'Please see that Miss Underhill gets this?'

'I will. What's the dog's name?'

'I guess it's Woofie.'

8

A Shot in the Dark

Promontory is comatose as we drive down the dark main street. We clear the town and cross the railroad tracks that divide city from county jurisdiction. The narrow gauge hasn't been used since the tannery closed 30 years ago, the railroad cars moldering away in the freight yard at the end of the line.

We come to a semi-rural intersection called Tannery Crossing. There's not much here except a few abandoned houses constructed for factory employees in the late 1800s. With their broken windows and sagging porches, they provide flops for the desperately homeless and drug-addicted. The five-story Franklin Hotel stands on the northeast corner of the intersection. A truncated fire escape terminates outside a third-story window, bleeding rust stains down the side of the building.

We pull to the curb across from the hotel. Standing in the entry is Fox Coat and three young women. He's wearing the plumed yellow hat Paula described. The women, skinny as straws, shiver in their thigh-high boots and mini-skirts. You couldn't make a decent chicken dinner if you threw all three of them in the pot.

As soon as Frack and I step from the car, the big man is on the move and the women scurry inside the lobby. He lumbers down the sidewalk toward the unlit parking lot, more earth-mover than race car, huffing and puffing by the time we catch up and spin him against the wall of the building.

It's immediately apparent that Fox Coat is physically incapable of marching through the frozen woods. He's just not the outdoorsy type. Frack turns him around and frisks him. He's clean. 'Why were you running?' says Frack.

'You were chasing me, man.'

'What's your name?' I ask.

'Baby Boy Clemson.'

'I mean your *real* name.'

'That's it. Ma died in childbirth, so the doc put down Baby Boy. Said my dad would name me when he picked me up, but he never came.'

'Ever hunt him down?'

'Didn't know who to look for. Why you two bracing me?'

'How old are you?' I continued.

'Twenty-seven. Been on my own since I was 14.'

'Your ladies seem pretty young to be in the business,' says Frack.

'They all got I.D.s. Not one of 'em is under 18.'

'That still doesn't make it legal to peddle their assets on the street. They got names?'

'Peaches, Cream Puff, and Angel Cake.'

'Delicious,' says Frack. I step on his toe and give it a little twist. He smiles but doesn't look at me. 'Your women could use warm clothes and a good meal.'

'I'll see to it, man. I promise.'

'This is a one-time pass,' I say. 'Tonight we're only interested in your coat, Mr. Clemson.'

'My coat? It's a genuine mink. I paid five hundred bucks for it.'

'Mind if I check the label?' says Frack.

'Knock yourself out.'

Frack folds down the back of the collar. 'It's from Elan Fashion Furs.'

'How did you come by it?' I say.

'Just a guy said his mom passed away and he needed money to pay for her funeral.'

'What did he look like?'

'Too dark to tell. Someone shot out the lights in the alley.'

'We're looking for the rest of them,' I say.

'The rest of what?'

'Coats. The other thirty-eight.'

'Thirty-eight! Whatchu talking about?'

There's a flash and a pop. I bounce against the building. A second bullet hits the wall and a chip of brick pings off my eyelid. I push Baby Boy to the sidewalk and reach for my gun. I pull off a single shot in the direction of the flash. I have no memory of taking aim, but when I hear a tortured howl like a coyote in a bear trap, I know I hit my target. It's the first time I've shot someone. It's the first time I've been shot.

Frack is pounding down the sidewalk with his gun out, but by the time he reaches the parking lot, the shooter's car is flying down the back alley. Frack runs back to where I stand bleeding. My left arm hangs uselessly and painfully at my side, but I'm still able to help Clemson to his feet with my right.

'We've got to get you to the E.R.,' says Frack.

'I got my mink dirty,' whimpers the big man.

'Doesn't matter,' says Frack. 'We're taking it with us. It's stolen.'

'What about my $500?'

'It's gone.'

Blood drips from my sleeve. I list in the wind. Frack puts his arm around me. 'How bad?' he says.

'I'm lightheaded.' At the sight of blood, the color drains from Baby Boy's face. 'Take a deep breath,' I tell him. 'Don't you dare faint on us.'

'There's a trail of blood in the parking lot,' says Frack. 'You hit your mark.'

'So did he,' I say. 'I guess we're even. Don't let Brooker stick me on a desk. I'll be fine.'

'I wouldn't worry about that right now,' he says, moving me toward the car.

A drop of red hits the top of my shoe. It's a flower with five petals unfolding from the center. 'Isn't that a poppy?' I say. Frack gives me a peculiar look. As my knees give way, he lifts me into his arms. A pale Baby Boy opens the car door and Frack sets me on the passenger seat. The fox coat settles over me like a fluffy cloud.

I look at Clemson. 'I want you . . . and your women . . . to be extra-careful until we figure out . . . '

Frack slams the door and climbs behind the wheel. I wilt against his shoulder. I feel blood running down my stomach. 'What is it we're trying to figure out again?' I ask, my tongue moving in slow motion.

'Nothing important,' he says. 'I'll take care of everything.'

We take off, tires smoking, my brachial artery spurting blood like a Roman fountain. Frack drives with one hand, compressing my wound with the other.

★　★　★

Marlis gets in late. She sees an envelope on the hall table with her name on it. She picks it up and opens it. Mark Alderman has left an itemized bill for Rommel's treatment: X-rays, shots, anesthesia, cast, etc. The balance comes to $560.

Across the front in red pen is written, 'Paid In Full.' She smiles and tucks the statement in her pocket. An excited whine comes from Miss Jennie's room and she peeks inside. Rommel pricks up his ears and snuggles closer to Miss Jennie. Between their Ace Bandages and plaster casts, they make a lovely pair.

9

A Tangled Web

I have no memory of Frack carrying me into the E.R. or of my vascular tank being three pints low on juice. I don't remember the tubes, the needles, the oxygen mask, or the bullet being dug out of my shoulder. The bullet? Well, maybe a little. When I come to, I'm in a hospital bed, floating high above my pain on a morphine drip. Now that I'm home, I've returned to earth with a painful thud.

After a week, I'm so bored I begin accepting Gladys's phone calls. I'd still be stuck at home if they weren't so short-handed at the station. Now I'm relegated to desk duty, and Big Mike is riding with Frack. I'm jealous and frustrated. I want my case back, but first I need a release from my primary care physician and therapist, Dr. Joel Weinstein, whom I have to see once a week.

Any nightmares or flashbacks?

Only about our sessions.

Very funny. Any depression or suicidal thoughts?

Hey, I'm a cop. We eat our guns like Popeye eats spinach.

How about feelings of guilt regarding the man you shot?

He shot me first, Weinstein. How guilty am I supposed to feel? Now sign my release.

No!

What a nincompoop! I can't help giving him a hard time.

Forensics took a sample of the shooter's blood from the parking lot, but it takes months to get DNA results back from the lab, provided we have the budget to send it in. The bullet went to ballistics, but aside from being a .22 we didn't learn much. There's no weapon to compare it with. We're not even sure if the shooter was aiming at us or Baby Boy Clemson.

The day after the shooting, Frack returned to the hotel. Clemson's little confections were all 18 or older, he had nothing to add about the person who sold him the coat, and he had no idea why anyone would want to shoot him. Frack gave the women the number of an organization that helps women get out of the sex trade. He told Baby Boy he'd only be getting a one-time pass on procuring charges. Next time he'd have to run faster.

In the meantime, leads on The Iceman Case are drying up. Frack tries to keep me up to speed on the investigation, but it's not the same as being directly involved.

It's shortly after lunchtime. I'm typing up Frack's report and finishing my fourth cup of coffee when an auburn-haired young woman walks into the station. She's catwalk-tall, with slender, shapely legs, auburn hair, and summer-blue eyes. I invite her to take the chair beside my desk.

'I'm Deputy Danner,' I say. 'How may I help you?'

She settles gracefully in the chair, a designer purse in her lap. She looks like the kind of woman who never drips coffee on her clothes or trips on a curb, unlike yours truly. 'I saw your picture in the paper when you got shot,' she says. 'I'm glad to see you're on the mend.'

'Thanks,' I say, rubbing my shoulder. 'I think I prefer gunplay. This typing is killing me.'

'I see you haven't lost your sense of humor. My name is Marlis Underhill. Jennie Lovelace says you were one of the deputies who came by when the branch came through the attic window.'

'You're the third roommate then. What can I do for you?'

'I'm concerned about someone who's gone missing.'

Marlis continues to tell me where she works, about the purse and the diary, and how Ruth Chambers's same-sex partner hasn't heard from her in almost a month — how no one has. 'This evening Ruth's sister Violet is having a few concerned parties to the house. They want me there. I know I'm popping this on you at the last minute, but would you consider joining us?'

'Have you gone to the local police?

That's the customary place to start.'

'They refuse to take a missing persons report. If you could just listen to what we have to say, maybe advise us on how to proceed, we'd appreciate it.'

'Okay, but I'm not sure how helpful I can be. Where and what time?'

'Eight.' Marlis writes down the address. She pulls an inhaler from her coat pocket and takes a couple pulls on it. 'It's my asthma,' she says. 'The cold gets me in the winter and the pollen in the summer.' Her hand is shaking.

'Is there something else you want to tell me about?'

There's a long pause. 'My imagination may be working overtime, but I think I'm being followed. I can't prove it, but I sense it.'

★   ★   ★

Dolly Markham isn't sure how long ago she took Mister under her wing. She found him standing by a dumpster in a downtown alley looking hungry and lost. He had a tangled bedhead and a briar patch of dark whiskers, and needed both a drink and a bath. She pulled a fifth of Jim Beam from her pocket and handed it over. He took a swig and handed it back. When she asked him his name and he couldn't come up with it, she figured it had something to do with his broken nose and the big lump on his head.

'I'm looking for my fur truck,' he said. 'I forgot where I left it.'

He was a little off like a lot of the homeless on the streets of Wausau. She was homeless too, but she still had her marbles. 'You know where the homeless shelter is?' she asked. He shook his head. 'How about the soup kitchen?' A blank stare. 'You come with me. I'll tell you everything you need to know.' She noticed how he kept patting the pocket of his coat. 'You need a cigarette? Me too.' She began pushing her shopping cart of bottles and cans. 'Well, come on. I think we have enough here to get us a pack of smokes.'

They'd been bumming around together ever since, hunting recyclables by day, sleeping in the shelter at night, eating at the soup kitchen, smoking. If she hadn't stumbled across him, he'd probably be frozen to death by now.

⋆ ⋆ ⋆

It's early evening when Sylvia arrives at Lovelace House, her eyes shining, a flush on her cheeks from the chill in the air. When she peeks into Jennie's room, the old lady sets her book aside. A big dog lying at her side lifts his head and wags a welcome.

'Come in, dear.'

'You have a big animal on your bed?'

'It's Woofie. I always knew he'd come home.' She studies the telltale glow on Sylvia's face. 'Why do I get the feeling you won't be with us much longer? Does it have something to do with that handsome Longtree boy?'

'In a couple weeks we're standing before the justice of the peace,' Sylvia answers. 'I'm giving my thirty-day notice. I hope you're not angry.'

'I could never be angry at you, dear. It's been a pleasure having you here.'

'I came to pack a suitcase. I'm going up north for a few days to visit my cousin, Luisa.'

'Well, drive carefully.'

'I will. I'm so pleased that Woofie is back home.'

'One thing before you go. I've been concerned about Rosalie. I'm not sure she's entirely well.'

'Now that she's not the center of my universe, she hates me. Don't waste your energy. She'll only suck you down a black hole.'

★ ★ ★

Her twin is standing at the boarded window when Sylvia steps into the attic. 'It's claustrophobic in here,' says Rosalie. She's looking somewhat pale and haunted. Sylvia pretends not to notice.

'Someone needs to call the handyman again and see if he can put in the new window. You need to let in the light,' says Sylvia, dragging her suitcase out of the closet, hoping to get in and out before they go at it again. She throws in a few warm outfits and clamps it shut.

'Where are you going?'

'Cousin Luisa needs my company for a few days.'

'That withered prune? What she needs is a husband.'

'I guess the right man hasn't come along yet.'

'But, yours has, right?'

'And yours will too.' Sylvia picks up her suitcase.

'When will you be back?'

'On April the third.'

'To Lovelace House or the Bar and Grill?'

'I've given Miss Jennie my notice,' Sylvia tells her.

'I despise you. You have no idea how much.' Rosalie's fists form tight little balls, her eyes burning like green match flames. 'You were the last person in the family I could count on. Now you don't care if I live or die.'

'It's hard to care about someone who doesn't care about herself.'

'You are such a pompous know-it-all.'

'I have to go,' says Sylvia, biting her

tongue. She turns to her sister one last time. 'Happiness is a choice, Rosalie,' she says, softening her tone. 'Life is full of disappointment. Most people find a way to rise above it. I'll see you when I get back.'

Rosalie is about to say something, but the door shuts and Sylvia is gone.

* * *

It's dark beyond the station window. Since the dog retrieved the wallet, the snow has begun to melt, and Frack and Mike have joined a party for one last search of the woods in case the remains of David Coburn are out there. Frack is so deep in the woods that our signal is weak and I strain to hear him.

'A searcher broke his leg in a fox hole,' shouts Frack over a rising wind. 'We're trying to get him to the road so I can drive him to the hospital.'

'I'm sorry to hear that. Anyone I know?'

'No. He's a volunteer out of New London. Mike's getting a ride home from one of the guys.'

'Did the search turn up anything significant?'

'A rusted wheelbarrow and the hub of an old wagon wheel.'

There's a groan from the injured searcher. 'Will you get off the damn phone?' he says. 'I got a bone poking through my skin.'

'Gotta go,' says Frack. 'I don't know when I'll be in. Have Gladys drive you home.'

He clicks off and I stare at the phone. You mean the Gladys who drove drunk with me when I was a baby? If I call her, she'll come with a bottle. I'll never get rid of her before the meeting at Violet Chambers's house, and I certainly can't bring her with me. I rotate my shoulder. There's a brief sound like the cracking of a knuckle. I was going to ask Frack to drive me to this evening's meeting, but I'll manage just fine.

Beyond the window, the wind whips the electrical wires between the power poles. A newspaper cartwheels down the sidewalk. I turn off the lights and lock up the station, then walk down the sidewalk past the closed store fronts, hunkered deeply inside my coat collar. I see my porch light in the distance and take a short cut across the town square. There is the dry snap of twigs in the darkness beneath the trees.

'Hello?' I say. No reply.

Something or someone crunches over the ice-crusted ground and I quicken my pace. I don't want Marlis Underhill's anxieties rubbing off on me, but I'm suddenly possessed of the urge to bolt like a rabbit. To my embarrassment, I run the last fifty yards to the house.

When I reach the gate, my ribs ache and my lungs are paralyzed with the cold. My red muffler is tied around the gate post, a sign that Tree Toppers has trimmed back the limbs where the no-neck cop set his speed trap. I snatch my muffler, swing through the gate, and go into the house through the back porch. Then I lock myself in and lean back against the kitchen door. My heart is still thundering when Fargo jumps up with comforting whines and kisses.

He trots up the stairs behind me. I look out of the bedroom window without turning on the light. Fargo jumps up and puts his paws on the sill. A man emerges from the shadows of the square with a short-legged dog. In the circle cast by the streetlamp, a match flares and ignites the tip of his cigarette. He looks up at the house through a swirl of smoke as if he knows he's being watched, his face obscured beneath the shadow of his hat. Fargo growls and presses his nose to the glass.

'Knock it off,' I say. 'You're freaking me out. He's just walking his dog.' Or is he? The fragment of a long-forgotten poem jumps unbidden into my head:

Walls have ears.
Wind spreads lies.
Trees know secrets.
Night has eyes.
Bolt the shutters.
Listen . . . wait . . .
What stranger watches
At my gate?

I change into jeans and a cable-knit sweater by the light filtering into the room from the hall. The next time I look, the man is gone.

★   ★   ★

I'm introduced to the women gathered at Violet's house. We chat casually for a few minutes over coffee. Violet is just home from her shift at the hospital, a focused, no-nonsense woman wearing her nurse's uniform and a stiff white hat. She's seated at the head of the dining room table with me at the opposite end. To my right is Marlis Underhill in a simple grey dress, and across the table sits Phyllis McCoy with Albert's widow, Julie Paxton.

'I'll begin,' says Violet. 'I found a photocopy of Ruth's car registration among her papers. The originals are in the glove compartment of her car, wherever that is. If it's located, it might provide a clue.'

I record the license and VIN numbers in my notebook and pass the copy back. 'I'd like each of you to tell me when you last made contact with Ruth, either in person or by phone,' I say.

Phyllis goes first. She's wearing orange again with turquoise jewelry. 'The night before Ruth vanished, we met for drinks at Vittoni's Bar in Appleton and made dinner plans to meet at the Olive Garden the following evening. The next day she called at around eleven to confirm our dinner date. When she didn't show and I couldn't reach her, I knew something was wrong. Violet hadn't seen her, so I called the yard the next morning. Bull said that he and Ruth had argued the previous day; she'd driven off and hadn't returned to pick up her paycheck.'

'Thank you, Phyllis,' I say. 'What about you, Julie?'

Julie fingers her pearl necklace. She's a well-dressed, silver-haired woman in her sixties. 'Ruth attended our Christmas party. Everyone from Bratton's was there. Ruth motioned me into the den. I thought she wanted to tell me something. In came Will with Claudine in tow. He carried two drinks, one for himself and another for Al. I found that odd, because

Al had been in his wheelchair near the fireplace all evening. 'I'll find him,' said Claudine, taking one of the drinks from Will and dancing from the room. Will gave Ruth a 'keep your mouth shut' look. I was called away and the moment passed. Al died that night. I never saw Ruth again, except from a distance at the funeral. I'll always wonder what she wanted to tell me.'

'That's consistent with the account in Ruth's diary,' says Phyllis.

'On December the 28th, a meeting had been scheduled between Al, our corporate lawyer and Will, who was supposed to bring documents pertaining to the business,' says Julie. 'He'd already cancelled twice, and with Al gone, the meeting never took place.'

'What happened to your husband's interest in the business?' I ask.

'There was a survivor policy. If one partner died, the other would acquire full ownership. At that point I was out of the picture. I guess I could have caused a legal ruckus, but I suspected Bull had already run the business into the ground.'

'Thank you, Julie,' I say. 'Phyllis, was there anything unusual about the evening at Vittoni's Bar?'

'Ruth was uncharacteristically quiet. I asked her if something was wrong. She said I was safer not knowing. One would usually say 'you'd be better off not knowing,' so I found the word 'safer' unsettling. Now I wish I'd pressed her harder.'

'Then you'd be missing too,' says Violet.

'If something was wrong, would it have been at work or at home?' I ask.

'She didn't get along with Bull, and she and Violet weren't on the same page in regard to our relationship.'

'Is that how you see it?' I ask Violet.

'We had our philosophical differences.'

'Julie, how was your husband's health when he and Mr. Bratton went into business?'

'Al had a little arthritis, but his general health was good for a man in his sixties. A few years later he was diagnosed with Crohn's Disease, an autoimmune disease of the digestive system. When he got sicker those last six months, I thought it was the stress of the partnership. His doctor kept upping the treatment, but Al kept getting worse.'

'Did you ask for an autopsy?'

'He was under the care of a physician, so it wasn't required. When a man has a legitimate illness, you're not focused on foul play. His doctor said, 'Julie, he's in his seventies. No one lives forever.''

'Thank you, Julie. Marlis, what do you do at the storage yard?'

'I was hired on a temporary basis to prepare Mr. Bratton for an upcoming IRS audit. It's been a nightmare. He has no filing system, just throws his documents in a grocery bag.' That gets a few smiles. 'Mr. Bratton made several unauthorized purchases after Mr. Paxton was too ill to work. I'd been told about Ruth's sudden departure from the job by a former employee, so when I found her purse in a filing cabinet, I knew something wasn't right.'

'Yes, but what?' says Violet.

'That's what we need to figure out,' says Phyllis.

I turn to Julie. 'Let's change gears for a moment. What was Mrs. Bratton like?'

'Claudine doesn't talk about herself. She doesn't have to. She looks like a centerfold and smells like money. When she was in Will's company, I got the feeling she'd rather be somewhere else — shopping, skiing, in the electric chair.' Everyone laughs. 'She and Bull are the mismatch of the century.'

'Anyone have a differing opinion?' No one did. 'Thank you, Julie. What about you, Violet? Did you see Ruth the morning she left for work on that last day?'

'I was in my room getting ready for my shift when I heard her drive away.'

'You've all read the diary. Is there something else we need to cover?'

'What did Ruth mean by crystals?' says Phyllis. 'How could the answer be in the crystals? The answer to what?'

'Is it even relevant?' says Violet.

'She thought it was,' says Phyllis.

'Aren't crystals used in healing, some New Age alternative medicine?' says Julie. 'Maybe she'd come across something to help my Al.'

'I don't think so,' says Violet. 'She was a born pragmatist and quite conventional — in most ways,' she says, cutting Phyllis a sharp-as-scissors glance. 'She mentioned the crystals after watching one of her crime shows. I could follow up on that and see where it leads.'

'That's an excellent idea,' I say.

'I'll report the car stolen,' says Violet. 'If the car is found, it might lead us to Ruth. We still need to file a missing persons report, but how can we do that if the police won't cooperate?'

'I'm told that Chief Bratton is Bull's brother,' I say.

'That's right,' says Violet. 'Bull is a blowhard, but Burgess is dangerous. Last year when Huey Sorensen ran against him for the office of chief, he was found a week before election day floating down the Fox River — under the ice. The case has never been solved; and since he was found in the Fox River and not the Little Wolf, it was investigated by the Appleton police.'

'And?'

'Sorensen had been bar-hopping. He

had a moderate level of alcohol in his system, so his death went down as an accidental drowning. Burgess was never even questioned.'

I can no longer avoid my next question. 'Does anyone here believe Ruth is alive?' I ask. The subsequent silence speaks for itself. 'Okay,' I say. 'We're going to pull the rug out from under the Promontory Police Department.'

'What does that mean?' says Marlis.

'The sheriff's department has jurisdiction over all homicides in the county, not the city police. There's enough circumstantial evidence to warrant a homicide investigation, but first I need the sanction of my senior officer.'

★   ★   ★

My left arm is throbbing as I drive one-handed through Promontory. With the leads dried up on The Iceman Case, I want to open an investigation into the disappearance of Ruth Chambers. I don't need a good arm to poke around and ask a few questions.

I'm halfway to Abundance when I see zigzagging headlights in my rear-view mirror. Within seconds, a black pickup is riding my bumper. I feel a nudge, then another, and my car fishtails. I'm suddenly wide awake, both hands on the wheel.

Another bump, this time harder. An escape route opens on the far side of the road. I fly across the left lane and pull into Burnt Barn Road, the truck still on my tail, the beams on high so I can't see the person behind the wheel. I don't have my shield with me, and my gun will remain locked in the safe until I'm released from desk duty.

There's a steep uphill slope to my left, a sharp drop-off to my right where the van went over, and a gate straight ahead. I'm hit hard from behind. My head snaps against the back of the seat. My forehead hits the steering wheel. I ride the brake as the truck pushes me forward. My only focus is keeping the car on the road.

The rusty gate comes at me like a medieval torture device. There's a screech of metal as it wraps around the grill, barbed wire scraping across the doors, posts snapping from the ground. A tire goes flat with a bang and I come to a stop. When I look behind me the truck is backing toward the main road. I'm already on the phone, dialing home.

Frack keeps me on the line as he races to my location. I throw the car door open and meet him halfway between the vehicles, my left arm drooping from my shoulder. I pour out my story and he holds me until I stop shaking.

'I didn't know what to think when I got home and you weren't there,' he says.

I step back from his embrace and search his face. 'What do you mean? I left a note taped to the microwave like I always do.'

'It's not important. Is Fargo okay?'

'He's at home,' I say.

The look on his face scares me. 'He's not there. I thought he was with you.'

'Oh, my god! What's happening?'

★ ★ ★

I fall asleep in Frack's arms, the one place in the world I know I'm safe from bullets and boogeymen and things that go bump in the night.

The next morning we drive our older car to the station. After I tell Mike about last night's meeting, he agrees to open a homicide investigation into Ruth Chambers's disappearance. I'm advised to proceed with caution. I could be stepping on some big toes.

I log onto my computer and run Wilbur Bratton's name through the National Crime Information Center. I'm disappointed when he comes back clean. That doesn't mean he *is* clean. It only means he's never been convicted of a crime.

'Isn't that your vehicle?' says Mike. I look up to see our car being towed down the street to Jim's Auto Repair. I tell him I hit a fence. It also explains the purple bump on my forehead.

'There's damage both front and rear,' he says. 'How did you manage that?'

'I was bumped into the fence from behind. I couldn't make out the plate.'

Mike isn't buying it, at least not all of it.

Frack looks at me across his desk. 'I

think we should call in a lost ad,' he says, shifting the focus of the conversation.

'What did you lose this time?' says Mike.

'Fargo has wandered off,' I say.

'I think I'll run off some flyers too,' says Frack. 'You think a reward of a hundred bucks is enough?'

'Yes,' I say. 'It's enough.'

'I know what I'm going to do today,' says Mike. 'A hundred dollars of diapers should last the triplets four whole days.'

We know the kids aren't in diapers anymore, but we have a good laugh anyway. Mike surprises me by walking to the safe and taking out my gun and shoulder holster. He holds them out to me. I look at him questioningly.

'Take them,' he says. I strap the holster on and snap the gun in place, trying not to flinch as a sharp pain runs down my arm.

'Does this mean I'm back on active duty?' I say.

'No. It means I don't know you removed the gun from the safe and I didn't notice when you went missing from behind your desk.'

'Thanks one hell of a lot.'

As I get in the patrol car and buckle up, I can breathe again. I have a gun. I have a job to do. I'm more than the daughter of the infamous Gladys Calhoun, although it will probably be memorialized on my tombstone. I slide my arm into the sling and drive one-handed toward Bratton Moving and Storage.

★   ★   ★

The shelter empties the homeless onto the street each morning. Dolly grabs her shopping cart and she and Mister head out for a day of can-hunting. Halfway down the block she stops.

'Mister, take a look at this,' she says, studying the missing persons flyer taped to the drugstore window. 'You got a twin brother out there?'

He doesn't reply, but focuses on the well-groomed fellow in the photo. Something tells him he's looked at that face before.

Dolly takes a position six feet behind

him. 'Hey, David!' she calls. He spins around. 'That's you.'

'Me?'

'Yes. Come on. We're going to the E.R.'

'Why? Are you sick?'

'No. We're going to get your identity back.'

★ ★ ★

I drive through the gates of the storage facility. It's not a sophisticated operation, just rows of shabby buildings secured by locks that could be knocked off by a ten-year-old with a hammer. It's clear that Claudine's millions don't trickle down to her spouse.

Marlis's car is parked in the garage next to a Caddy. A muscular white dog on a chain announces my arrival with crazy-eyed snorts and snarls. I park near a door that says 'Office,' and leave my sling in the car so I don't look like the walking wounded.

Marlis is being berated by a thick-necked man with a red face and broken veins across his nose. He's a less fit version of Burgess Bratton.

'That vet of yours wanted $560 for treating Rommel. Why should I pay that kind of money when I can have him euthanized for $50?'

'You have a point, Mr. Bratton.'

'I told him he can keep the damn dog. He's not getting a dime from me.'

'I didn't mean to upset you. You'll have my resignation on your desk in five minutes.'

'Oh no!' he says. 'You have work to do, Miss Underhill.'

Marlis flicks me a glance and a half-smile as she walks out the door. Bratton looks over at me. 'You're that lady cop.'

'I'm Deputy Danner, Mr. Bratton.'

'Can I get you a cup of coffee?'

'No, thanks.'

'You got a bump on your forehead. Someone punch you?'

'No one who isn't in a cooler at the morgue.'

'You're joking, right?'

'Yes, I'm joking.'

'How may I help you? Keep in mind

I'm pressed for time.'

'Just a few questions and I'll be out of your hair.'

'You catch one of my boys speeding?'

'No, sir. This is in regard to a woman who was formerly in your employ. A Miss Ruth Chambers.'

'Not that again! I haven't seen the woman since she quit. That was weeks ago. First her lesbo friend calls, then her sister the shrew. What do people want from me?'

'Can you tell me the circumstances surrounding Miss Chambers's departure?'

'She wanted things done her way. I want things done my way. As they say, the boss isn't always right, but the boss is always the boss.'

'So you argued the day she left. What time was that?'

'Around lunchtime. She left and never returned. We'd fought before and she always came back, so I was surprised when she didn't come back this time to pick up her paycheck.'

'Where were you when you had this little tiff?'

'Here in my office. Then we took it outside as she headed for her car.'

'Did she leave with her purse?'

'What kind of question is that? Men don't notice that kind of thing.'

'Did she go to her office before she left?'

'She went straight to her car.'

'So she had her car keys with her.'

'They're always in her pocket.'

'Did you threaten her?'

'Of course not.'

'A man your size can appear quite intimidating even if he doesn't intend to.'

'I'm big. There's not a hell of a lot I can do about that.'

'How about phone calls or visitors that day?'

'One call to the lesbo. One from my wife. No visitors.'

'Her final paycheck, Mr. Bratton. You still have it?' He rifles through the clutter in a drawer beneath the counter and hands it to me. 'How about the checkbook it came from?' He scrounges around again and hands it to me. I'm satisfied that it was written in sequence and made out the day before payday with the rest of the payroll. 'Thank you.' I hand it back.

A Promontory police car pulls into the lot. The dog goes nuts again.

'You know that dog presents a liability, Mr. Bratton. If he attacks someone, you could be in deep trouble.'

'Yeah, Jack might be a bit more dog than I expected.'

The door opens and Chief Bratton walks in. He wears his signature western boots and a cowboy hat. A big nightstick swings from his belt. 'Not you again,' he says.

'Good morning, Chief,' I say pleasantly.

'What are you doing here?'

'I'm investigating the disappearance of Miss Ruth Chambers.'

'What disappearance? She hangs out at the Ho-Chunk Casino in Nakoosa.'

'You got video, I'd like to see it. You so much as sneeze and the casino has it on film.'

'It's not your concern. She's a resident of Promontory.'

'She disappeared from here. Deputy Oxenburg has opened an investigation.'

'You can't do that. If it's anyone's case, it's ours.'

'I know of at least two people who've tried to get that done, sir. They were both stonewalled by your department. Besides, it's gone from a missing persons case to a homicide investigation. That puts it under our jurisdiction.'

'A homicide investigation? You can't be serious.'

'How many times have you walked off a job without picking up your check?' He opens his mouth, but nothing comes out. 'That's what I thought. Me neither.' I turn my attention back to Wilbur. 'Are any of your men around?'

'They're all out. They should be back in a couple hours.'

'I'd like the names, addresses and phone numbers of anyone working here during Miss Chambers's employ. Actually, photocopies of their job applications will do as long as their information is still valid.' He attacks a second messy drawer. 'Make sure you don't forget anyone.'

I ask a few more questions as he photocopies the papers. As I glance around the walls, I see a framed certificate. 'You were a pilot?' I ask.

'I *am* a pilot. My wife Claudine and I met at the flight club.'

He's sweating when he hands me the aps. Included with each one is a photocopied snapshot of the applicant. 'You require a photo?' I ask.

'Claudine doesn't want me hiring any guys that aren't full-blooded Americans.'

'You mean they have to be Potawatamis or Menominees?'

'I think you know what I mean.'

I hand him my card with my cell phone number written on the back. 'If you have a sudden epiphany, please give me a call.'

'Wait a minute,' says Chief Bratton. 'Can't we compare notes before you go off the deep end with this Ruth Chambers thing?'

'Have a good day, Chief.'

The moment I close the door, Marlis steps from her office and motions me over. 'I listened in to Bull and Burgess arguing over the phone this morning. Bull wants Burgess to empty storage unit number twenty. Burgess was furious. Bull told him if he doesn't, he's putting his trash in the Dumpster.'

'Do you know what's in the unit?'

'No, but I bet I can find a key when Mr. Bratton isn't looking.'

'Don't go near that unit. One missing person is all I can handle right now. Any idea why Will doesn't want to store his brother's possessions?'

'The chief doesn't think he should have to pay storage like everybody else.'

'Talk about a sense of entitlement!'

I'm not sure that Wilbur Bratton has done more than perfect the art of being crude and unlikeable, which of course is not a crime. Then again, if Chief Bratton refused to investigate the disappearance of Ruth, he may have his own suspicions regarding his brother.

I drive slowly back toward Abundance, checking the woods and ditches along the road for any sign of Fargo. Is he dead or alive? Is he hungry and cold? There's a big echoing void in our lives that only a big goofy dog can fill.

★　★　★

Frack and I hook up at the Bluebird for lunch. 'Any news on Fargo?' I say.

'Not yet, but I called in the ad and the flyers are up.'

'That's good. What's the smile for?' I ask him.

'David Dorne Coburn is alive.'

'Alive?' I set my coffee down before I spill it.

'We got a call from the Wausau Police Department. Coburn has been staying in the homeless shelter right there in town. He's suffered a serious concussion and a broken nose; can't remember his name or what happened to him.'

'Traumatic amnesia.'

'Yes. The doctor says it's a temporary condition, but he may never remember the attack itself.'

'So now we're looking for the person who stole the furs from the person who stole them first.'

'That's about the size of it. What did you learn at Bratton's?'

I give him the rundown and show him

the copies of the job aps I brought back with me. My cell vibrates. It's Violet Chambers calling from the hospital. We talk briefly and click off.

'That was Ruth's sister. She wants me to come to her place around five thirty when she gets off duty. She has something to tell me, but not over the phone.'

'Fine, but this time you're not going alone,' says Frack.

'I don't want to go alone.'

I spend the rest of the day running the Bratton employees through the database. I talk with their neighbors, former employers and personal references, but no red flags go up. Benny Goddard didn't have as much as a parking ticket. Hank Logan had a five-year-old DWI. Around the same time he was involved in a bar fight, but the charges were dropped. Even Wilbur 'Bull' Bratton comes up with nothing more serious than two past bankruptcy filings. Big surprise.

On impulse, I tap in the name Claudine du Lac Bratton. She and Wilbur married six years ago. I go to the online Appleton Post Crescent and scroll back in time. Claudine has always been a star in the society section and covered extensively in gossip columns. She couldn't walk out her front door without being memorialized in print.

One particular piece stands out.

POPULAR SOCIALITE WEDS

Two months after the untimely loss of her parents, socialites Genevieve and Jean-Rene, Claudine du Lac, heiress to granite quarry millions, breaks off her long-term engagement to attorney Michael T. Anderson and weds businessman Wilbur Arthur Bratton. When Miss du Lac was twelve, she lost her older sister Patrice in a tragic accident at the family home, etc. etc.

'We'd better get going,' says Frack. 'You can finish that in the morning.'

When I look up, Big Mike is gone. In the distance, the sun has dropped beneath the pine trees and a thick mist rises from the banks of the Little Papoose.

We drive toward Promontory with

Frack at the wheel. We pass through the woods where I hunted Indian arrowheads and collected pinecones as a child. I'll never be that child again, and the woods will never be those woods.

'You okay?' says Frack.

'I'm frustrated. We're out of leads on The Iceman Case. The DNA results on the blood sample from the parking lot won't be back for months, even if we find the money in the budget to send it in. I can't get a handle on Ruth Chambers's disappearance, and I want Fargo back home where he belongs, hogging the bed and eating us out of house and home.'

Violet has the door open as soon as we get out of the car. Julie and Phyllis are here, but I don't see Marlis. I introduce Frack to the group.

'Where's Marlis?' I say.

'We called the house, but no one picked up.'

We gather around the table.

'Today I invited myself to lunch with gastroenterologist Dr. Noah Staley,' says Violet. 'I showed him Ruth's diary entry and asked if he saw a correlation between crystals and Al's illness. When I think of crystals, I think of jewelry. Staley thinks of kidneys.'

'Kidneys?' I say.

'Yes. People who are poisoned with ethylene glycol develop crystals in the kidneys.'

'Ethylene glycol? That's antifreeze,' says Frack.

'That's right,' says Violet. 'It's tasteless, odorless and very deadly. Two to three ounces is considered a fatal dose. I think this is the connection Ruth stumbled on.'

'Since Al had already been diagnosed with Crohn's Disease, his doctor didn't think it unusual when his symptoms worsened,' says Julie. 'What if Al was given antifreeze in small doses over time, and finished off with a fatal dose on Christmas night? One would assume he died of Crohn's.'

'Who had access to Al other than you, Julie?' I ask. 'It would have been someone able to poison his food or drink over a period of time.'

'Friends. Neighbors. Relatives. Employees from the yard. He had a lot of visitors.

It would be hard to narrow down, because he's not the kind of person to make enemies.'

'It had to be someone with a motive — love, money or revenge,' I say. 'Someone who would have benefitted from his death in some way.'

'I guess that would be me,' says Julie. 'I'm the beneficiary of his $200,000 life insurance policy, so I'd be seen as suspect number one. He left trusts for our two grown children, but they live out of state. Will gets Al's half of the business, but if Wilbur had died first, Al would have acquired Will's half.'

'Except Wilbur didn't die first,' says Frack.

'If Julie makes a request, Dr. Staley will order a disinterment and post-mortem,' says Violet. 'If crystals are found, it becomes a homicide investigation.'

'Are you prepared to consider that?' I ask Julie.

'I owe that much to Al. You know, there's something that struck me as odd at the time. Will and Claudine arrived for a visit a couple weeks before Albert passed away. They brought shakes and cheeseburgers. They always bring lunch when they visit. Will passed out the food. When he gave Al his shake, Claudine snatched it up and said, 'Oops, that's Julie's,' and made a switch.'

Frack and I exchange a glance. 'Were they the same flavor?' he asks.

'I can't remember. That night Al became violently ill, but he was ill to one degree or another all the time. I always noticed that being around Will exacerbated his symptoms.'

'You mean they didn't get along?' says Frack.

'Will does not have a natural acumen for business. We'd hired a corporate lawyer to go over the books. We were probably headed toward a lawsuit, but the three of us remained civil. As for Claudine, she had nothing to gain from Al's death. She has her own money and plenty of it.'

On the way back to Abundance, my throbbing arm back in the sling, I close my eyes and let the miles slip by with Frack behind the wheel. I'm dozing when my cell phone jolts me awake, sending a spasm of pain shooting from my shoulder to my fingertips.

Bratton Moving and Storage appears on the caller I.D. My first thought is Marlis and I click on. 'Deputy Danner here.'

I straighten up, fully awake now. It's Will Bratton panting into the phone like a fat man running a 5K. In the background the yard dog is barking and thrashing his chain. 'You've got to get out here right away or . . . '

There's a gunshot and a high-pitched shriek. It's impossible to tell if it's human or canine.

'Mr. Bratton? *Mr. Bratton?*'

I hear his phone hit the ground.

* * *

The basement is dark and cold. Fargo lies as close to the water heater as he can without catching his tail on fire. In the morning the woman puts fresh water in his bowl and kibbles in his dish beside the dryer. She doesn't talk to him. She doesn't pat his head. Every evening the man in the uniform opens the door and looks down at him from the top of the stairs.

'You're a fool to do that man's bidding,' says the woman. 'If he's so brave let him hide the animal.'

'He's my boss. What can I do?'

'My sister in Arizona says they're interviewing in Phoenix. You don't want to be collateral damage when everything falls apart — and it will.'

'It's not like I know anything specific.'

'If this ends up on our doorstep, I'm leaving you.'

Fargo can't understand the words but he knows they're talking about him. He misses the man who walks him in the woods and the woman whose eyes are gentle and soft when she looks at him. He misses pizza and chocolate cake and his Raggedy Ann doll. He wants to go home.

10

Everything Hits the Fan

Frack hears the gunfire erupt through my phone.

'There's trouble at Bratton's,' I say. The car jumps forward. I discard my sling and unbutton my coat to make my gun easily accessible.

We're driving the family car. Neither of us is wearing our bulletproof vest or carrying handcuffs. We hit 70 mph on an empty stretch of road, our destination only minutes away. We pass through the thickest section of woods, the fragmented moon peering through the windblown branches of maple and pine. I tap in a quick call to the state police for backup and give them our location.

'Slow down,' I say as the Bratton sign comes into view. The gate is open and we fly through it, scraping the undercarriage and sending up a shower of sparks. My senses are on high alert, my blood electric with adrenaline. Headlights from an idling van illuminate a man on the ground. He tries rising on an elbow, blood pooling on the ground beneath him. I can't tell which no-neck brother it is, and my first thought is that someone has been attacked by the white dog. As I try to make sense of what I'm looking at, a man in a cowboy hat runs across the yard and leaps into the van. It's Burgess Bratton.

The yard dog goes berserk and snaps his chain. The chief yanks the door handle of the van but the dog is already airborne, locking his teeth on a bulging thigh. Burgess reaches for his nightstick but can't free it from the loop at his waist. He lets out a horrific bellow as the dog thrashes his head from side to side, ripping through muscle and fat.

Frack and I are out of the car, Frack's gun leveled at Burgess. I grab the dog's collar. The animal has more strength in his neck than I have in my whole body. I twist and pull his back leg until he loses his footing and tumbles backward to the ground.

Dragging a length of chain behind him, he circuits the yard, coming to rest beside Will. Frack drags Burgess from the van, disarms him and slaps him against the side panel. He howls and clutches his savaged leg.

I run over and drop beside Will, avoiding eye contact with the dog, whose breath is warm and smells of blood. I'm not looking for a reason to shoot him — the dog, that is — although it doesn't seem a bad idea given his propensity for mayhem.

'Lie still. Stop trying to get up, Mr. Bratton.'

'The s.o.b. tried to kill me. My own brother.'

I help him out of his coat and ease him onto his back, using my muffler as a tourniquet. The bullet that entered his arm isn't a through-and-through, suggesting it's lodged against bone.

Will looks at the blood on the ground. 'Am I going to die?' he says evenly.

'Maybe in twenty years if you don't quit the smokes.'

'Very funny.' I see the painful trace of a smile. He grits his teeth and forcefully blows out his breath. No moaning. No tears of self-pity. Gotta give him credit for knowing how to take a bullet like a man.

'You're a tough customer, Mr. Bratton. Want to tell me what's going on?' I can see by the defeated look in his eyes that he's ready to give up what he knows.

'Burgess told me he had camping equipment in number twenty. I told him he either pays the storage fee or I toss his trash. He laughed in my face. After he left, I unlocked the unit and found piles of fur coats. He didn't trust me not to snoop. He came back and flew into a rage. I pulled out my phone. He pulled out his gun. I was quicker on the draw, but my phone was out of bullets. He got me good. He loaded the coats in the van while I lay bleeding like a stuck pig. It's the same van he borrowed the day of the heist.'

'And your part in all this? You damn well better tell me the truth.'

'Listen, lady, I found out on the news

like everybody else.'

'I'm locking your dog up, Mr. Bratton. Animal Control will pick him up in the morning.' Guilt washes over Will's face as he looks at the animal he'd treated so poorly, the animal who watches so steadfastly over him now.

A state police car pulls into the yard, followed by an ambulance. Burgess is slumped against the van, standing on one leg like a 250 lb. stork. His other leg is missing a piece of flesh the size of a rump roast.

'Do me a favor,' says Will. 'I need someone to drive my car to the hospital.'

'We can manage that.'

'It's the yellow Caddy. The keys are in the ignition. Drop them at the desk in the E.R.'

'You're pretty bossy for a wounded man.'

He's still giving orders when the ambulance door slams shut.

The state policeman takes charge of Burgess Bratton, administering first aid and preparing to transport him to the hospital ward of the county jail. It looks like we'll be working the case together. Frack follows Will's ambulance in the Caddy and I trail along in the car.

★ ★ ★

Before we climb into bed, I call Marlis. I tell her about the meeting at Violet's and the shooting at the yard.

'I was expecting something to blow,' she says. 'There's no shortage of bad blood between those two.'

'Wilbur's in the hospital, so you'll have to decide about tomorrow.'

After a pause, she says: 'I'll go to work. I know the system well enough to keep things hanging together until Mr. Bratton returns.'

'My friend, you are a saint.'

★ ★ ★

The next morning Frack gets ready to meet with the state policeman for Burgess Bratton's bedside interrogation. 'You coming?' he asks.

'We don't need two cops doing a

one-cop job,' I say. 'I'm working the Chambers case.'

'Good luck,' he says. He gives me a kiss and drops me off at the station.

I'm on my computer when Mike walks in. 'Where's your limp, Big Guy? You're looking pretty steady on your feet this morning.'

'I'm fit as a fiddle. The crocuses are up in the garden and spring is in the air. I've been on the horn with the state police all morning. You two had quite a night.'

'We have our suspect in The Iceman Case, but we've got a long way to go before we put him away. Bratton's nightstick is a perfect match to the bruise on the victim's throat.'

'I wouldn't miss today's interrogation for all the tea in China,' he says.

'You'd better get going then. Frack's got the jump on you.'

★   ★   ★

Since Claudine du Lac married Wilbur Bratton, her former fiancé, Michael Anderson, Esquire, has gone from private practice to lead prosecutor at the state capitol. I call ahead and we meet for lunch at The Hung Jury across from city hall. Anderson is tall and blond, a Robert Redford look-alike in a crisp grey suit and mauve silk shirt with French cuffs. He's a type-A personality who can't stop looking at his watch. We sit across from one another at a window table. Another glance at the watch. I smile and he smiles back.

'Sorry,' he says. 'I don't mean to be rude, but I'm arguing a case in half an hour.'

He has the waiter bring shrimp cocktail and iced tea. It's quick. Chop. Chop. Chop. Mr. Anderson is a man on the fast track.

'So, what can I do for you, Deputy Danner?'

'What can you tell me about Claudine du Lac?'

'What has she done now?' he says matter-of-factly.

'That's a telling response, Mr. Anderson.'

'Like I said, I only have' — he looks at

his watch — 'twenty-three minutes before I turn into a pumpkin.'

'Miss du Lac broke your engagement and married a gentleman with whom she has absolutely nothing in common. How do you account for that?'

'Correction — *I* broke off the engagement.'

'You?'

'The people closest to Claudine have uncharacteristically bad luck. Her sister Patrice drowned in the family pool one month short of her eighteenth birthday when she would have inherited multi-millions from her grandparents. She and Claudine were the only ones home at the time. Claudine was twelve, spoiled and headstrong. Patrice's money eventually went to Claudine along with her own share. Three months before our wedding date, her parents crashed their plane on a short run in good weather. Claudine is the one who saw them off at the airport where Mr. Bratton kept his Piper Apache. She fell ill at the last minute and stayed behind. The plane crashed and she became the last apple on the du Lac family tree.'

'That's some story. You should sell it to Hollywood.'

'Except there's no Hollywood ending. Her parents were philanthropists. Their philosophy differed from Claudine's; she wanted the fortune to remain intact. They were about to pledge two million dollars to be used for a children's hospital wing. With them gone, Claudine declined to honor the agreement, nor did she have a legal obligation to do so.' He sets down his fork. 'She did something to the plane. The man she married knows what. He always watched her, even when she didn't know he was there. She wouldn't wipe her riding boots on the man and suddenly he's walking her down the aisle with a big smile and no pre-nup.'

'No pre-nup? That doesn't sound like the Claudine you describe.'

'I think that's the point.' He lifts a finger and the waiter appears. 'Miss Danner has had a long drive, Henry. Make sure she gets a nice lunch and put it on my tab.'

'As you wish, sir.'

Anderson slides his chair back and tosses his napkin on the table. 'Connect the dots, Deputy. I wish you luck.'

'Thank you, Mr. Anderson. Good luck with your case.'

I watch him go out the door, trot across several lanes of lunch hour traffic, and bound up the steps of city hall.

★   ★   ★

Spring has not yet arrived in Manitowish Waters. The lake is frozen solid, snow tucked between the gables of the inn like frosting on a cake. Since surgery, Cousin Luisa feels better than she has in years. She and Sylvia have never laughed so hard or drunk so much champagne.

The Inn is their peaceful hideaway until the boom of the iron door knocker echoes through the halls. They approach the door a bit tipsy and apprehensive. 'Maybe it's Jack Nicholson after all,' says Sylvia. They giggle nervously.

'I hope it's John Dillinger,' says Luisa. 'I'll hide him in my bedroom closet.'

'I'll hide him in my bed,' says Sylvia.

They burst out laughing. 'Will you open the goddamn door? It's freezing out here.'

'Oh god!' says Luisa. 'It's my mother. I'm going to kill myself.' She plasters a smile on her face and opens the door. 'Mother!'

'Aunt Cecile!' says Sylvia.

Cecile lugs her suitcase inside and Luisa pushes the door shut. 'Where's the help? Who's going to carry my bag?'

'They have a few days off,' Luisa explains. 'I wanted time to myself.'

'What's Sylvia doing here?'

'Keeping me company. How did you get here?'

'With great difficulty. I suppose you put her in the Rose Room.'

'There are dozens of other rooms, Mother. How about the Pocahontas Suite?'

'I suppose it will do.' She turns to Sylvia. 'How long will you be staying now that the cavalry has arrived?' It's obvious that 20,000 square feet is not enough space to accommodate both Sylvia and her aunt.

'I'll be leaving earlier than planned.'

'Of course you will, dear.'

211

Sylvia isn't expected home until the third. Now she'll surprise Kent on April Fool's Day.

* * *

The man and woman are fighting again. No one has fed him today or looked at him from the top of the stairs. There are wiggly things in his water bowl.

'Are you waiting until they arrest you for being an accessory after the fact?'

'What do you expect me to do, Eleanor?'

'You know what I expect.' She shoves a deer rifle in his hand. 'Take him into the woods. It's not like he's worth anything.'

* * *

Driving back from the capitol, I bypass the Abundance turnoff and go straight to the hospital. The bullet has mushroomed against Wilbur Bratton's humerus and he's scheduled for surgery in an hour.

When he sees me he rolls his eyes. 'You again,' he says.

'You weren't complaining last night.'

'You won't let my brother out on bail so he can finish the job, will you?'

'I don't think bail is an option. Are you up to answering a few questions?'

'No.'

'I'll take that as a yes. Has your wife been in to see you?'

'No.'

'How about a phone call?'

'This is her spa day.'

'I understand that you and Claudine visited Al when he was sick.'

'So? I was a lousy partner but I liked him.'

'And you brought fast food.'

'I also brought girlie magazines and Schnapps if Julie wasn't around. Is that your question?'

'During one visit, milkshakes were placed on the table. Claudine switched Julie's and Al's, saying, 'Oops! That's not right,' or something to that effect. Do you recall that event?'

'Claudine was confused. Julie sometimes ordered chocolate, but that day we all had vanilla.'

'So it wouldn't matter who got what.'

'That's right.'

'We're looking into Al's death as a possible homicide.'

'Homicide? He died of Crohn's.'

'Mr. Bratton, can you tell me if your marriage to Claudine du Lac is 100% satisfactory?'

'Lady, nothing in my life is 10% satisfactory. I've got a bullet in my arm, the IRS is breathing down my neck, and my business is failing.'

'It hasn't gone unnoticed that you and Claudine are an unlikely couple.'

'So were Sophia Loren and Carlo Ponti.'

'I understand you were at the airport the day her parents' plane went down.'

'I kept my plane there long before she came along.'

'She was scheduled to be on that flight.'

'I guess. She got sick at the last minute. Who wants to throw up at fifteen hundred feet?'

'Mr. Bratton, I think you know why that plane crashed. I also believe you're not the kind of man to pass on an opportunity.'

The nurse enters the room. 'Sorry,

Deputy Danner. I have to start the I.V.'

'I'm leaving just now. Tell the surgeon to save the bullet. We need it for ballistics. And think about what I said, Mr. Bratton. I have a feeling you'd like to get the elephant off your chest.'

*　*　*

Rosalie flips through the hangers on Sylvia's side of the closet. Her sister has already moved much of her wardrobe to the Bar and Grill, but it will take another carload to get everything. If she's going to pass as Sylvia, she should wear something Kent has seen before. Nothing too sexy. Nothing too boring. She decides on a red cashmere sweater, blue jeans and a pair of Sylvia's gold butterfly earrings. She checks the date on the calendar. It won't be long before she pulls off the most brilliant April Fool's caper ever.

*　*　*

The next morning Benny and Hank arrive at the yard shortly after Marlis. She explains why Will won't be coming in. Everyone decides to make it a regular working day. The scene of the shooting has been processed, the evidence removed from storage unit #20, the yellow tape broken and rippling in the wind. At nine o'clock Jack is taken away by Animal Control. Marlis spends the day posting payments, scheduling pick-ups and answering phones.

It's dark when she walks through the door of Lovelace House and peeks in on Miss Jennie and Woofie.

'Come in, Marlis. We heard about the shooting. Are you safe down there?'

'Yes. All the excitement is over. Can I get you something before I go up?'

'Rosalie has already walked Woofie and made me a TV dinner. Healthy Choice. It wasn't half as bad as you might imagine.'

'I'm glad she's taking good care of you.'

'Come to think of it, there is something you might do. Can you take Woofie to his follow-up appointment when the time comes? The doctor doesn't want me driving for a couple more weeks.'

'Yes, of course.' Marlis smiles at the prospect of seeing Mark Alderman again.

'Thank you, dear.'

Marlis is halfway up the stairs when her phone vibrates. She pulls it out of her coat pocket. 'Hello.'

'This is Claudine Bratton.'

'Yes, Claudine. How is Mr. Bratton doing?'

'He's still in the hospital. I feel terribly alone tonight. Can you join me for dinner?'

She's surprised by the invitation. It's not like she and Claudine are ever going to move in the same social circles.

'I hope you like game hen and wild rice.'

'I don't mean to hesitate, but I've just walked in the door and I'm dying to get out of my high heels.'

'Good, you haven't eaten then. Dinner will be ready in half an hour. We're the only house on Lakeside Drive.'

Marlis would rather nuke a Top Ramen and put her feet up, but she's curious about the big stone edifice that Missy Fisher couldn't stop raving about.

After a long day I make a sandwich and warm a can of soup. I'm settled in front of the TV when Frack calls. 'I have to make it quick,' he says.

'How did the interrogation go?'

'When Mike and I walked in the room, Bratton had already lawyered up, but he won't be granted bail. We're still reviewing the evidence with the D.A. so I'll be late.'

'We'll talk in the morning then.'

After we click off I call the hospital. The bullet in Wilbur's arm was successfully removed, but an infection has set in. If he shows improvement he can go home in a day or two. I pour a second cup of coffee and call Marlis.

'Hello.'

'Marlis?'

'No, it's Rosalie. Marlis forgot her phone when she left.'

'You mean this morning?'

'No, after work. Mrs. Bratton called and asked her to the chateau for dinner.'

'That was rather late notice.'

218

'That's what I thought.'

'Thank you, Rosalie. By the way, have you had that attic window fixed yet?'

'The handyman is still coming, but since the blizzard a few other jobs have taken priority.'

'Be sure you don't let him blow you off.'

* * *

Chateau du Lac sits on a dead end road on the shores of Little Papoose Lake. It's a Norman manor house with a conical tower on each end of the stone façade. A boathouse stretches over the water. It houses a sleek outboard and the high-end jet-ski Mr. Bratton denied purchasing. There's a runway behind the house and a red-striped Piper Apache sitting in a metal hangar.

Marlis walks up the flagstone path and rings the bell. Claudine opens the door with a Hollywood smile. 'Come in,' she says. 'Let me take your coat.' She hangs it in the hall closet. 'I'm so glad we're finally meeting face to face.'

'Your house is lovely. I've never seen anything quite like it.'

'And you won't unless you move to France. Daddy had it moved stone by stone from Champagne, but Mother put her foot down when he suggested a moat. I guess he thought the lake needed one more place to hatch mosquitos.'

Marlis laughs. She's changed into a velvet pants suit and comfortable flats. Claudine is equally casual in a white silk blouse, brown jodhpurs and riding boots.

'Something smells wonderful.'

'I'm just going to take dinner out of the oven,' Claudine says, walking toward the kitchen.

'Can I help?'

'The dining room is that way. Pick a chair where you can see the lights across the lake and I'll be right with you.'

★   ★   ★

'It was a lovely dinner *and* a beautiful view,' says Marlis as they finish their after-dinner coffee.

'How about another slice of cheese-cake?'

'Thank you, but I couldn't eat another bite.'

'We could share a bottle of extra-dry sauvignon blanc.'

Marlis looks at her watch. 'Missy raved about your famous wine cellar, but I'm afraid I must be getting back.'

'If you have ten minutes, I'll give you a lightning tour of the netherworld of Chateau du Lac. The Count of Monte Cristo has escaped, but there are still a few points of interest.'

'All right, you've talked me into it.'

Claudine pulls a medieval-looking iron key from her pocket and unlocks an equally ancient door at the end of a long hall. A flight of hand-carved stone steps leads downward into a pool of darkness at the bottom. Claudine flicks a switch and a dim light goes on in the cellar. The draft blowing up from below is frigid and Marlis hugs herself as they descend.

'You should have grabbed your coat. I got used to the chill years ago.'

The cellar is exactly as Missy described

— hundreds of bottles of wine in tall racks along the walls, three chest freezers, boxes of household supplies, and stores of food. Beneath the wine rack, Marlis catches a glint of metal.

'I think someone dropped a coin,' she says. 'Probably the count.' She leans over and picks it up. 'Look, it's a set of car keys.'

'I've been looking for those.' Claudine smiles and holds out her hand. Marlis hands them over but not before she notices the R.C. engraved into the attached medallion. Now she remembers what had been nagging at her. It was something Claudine had said when they first spoke: 'I haven't seen Ruth since the day she quit.' The day she quit?

R.C. Ruth Chambers. No one knows Ruth met anyone that day. Marlis's chest tightens. 'I need to go back up. My inhaler's in my coat pocket, but I'd love a raincheck.'

'Any time.'

As Marlis starts up the steps, Claudine pulls a bottle from the rack. A glancing blow comes down on Marlis's head and she crumples to the stones at the bottom of the steps.

'I was afraid you'd remember that conversation,' says Claudine to the motionless figure. 'Funny how one little misstep can screw things up.' She returns the unbroken bottle to the rack, glad she hadn't shattered one of the best years for cabernet. She avoids the slowly spreading blood around Marlis's head, climbs the stairs and exits the door at the top of the flight. She locks it behind her. She'd never dreamed — way back when — that things would become this complicated. Then again, murder is never as simple as you want it to be.

* * *

Will gets out of bed and looks down the hall. It's very quiet, the nurses chatting at their station. He pulls on his street clothes and exits through the emergency door across from his room. His car is waiting in the parking lot just like the lady cop promised.

After a twenty-minute drive, he pulls

into a grove of trees on Lakeside Drive and enters the chateau grounds on foot. He wonders why Marlis Underhill's green Chevy is parked out front. When women get together you never know what they'll cook up. Whatever it is, it's never good.

He walks up the hill to the hangar before turning on his flashlight. As he looks at his beloved Piper Apache, his thoughts rewind to the sunny, cloudless day at the airport when his life took a serendipitous turn — or so he thought back then.

★   ★   ★

'I can't believe I left our thermoses back at the house,' says Genevieve du Lac.

'There's a lunch counter in the terminal,' offers Claudine. 'Why don't you two grab some coffee while I fuel up?'

'You fuel the plane?' says Jean-Rene.

'Don't be so controlling,' says Genev-ieve. 'She's every bit as qualified as you are.'

As her parents walk away, their daughter leans against the hangar, her blonde hair shining, her pretty face turned to the sun. Wilbur stands behind his Apache two spaces down. He can't stop obsessing over the rich du Lac girl, even after she announced her engagement to that pompous lawyer. He waits for her to fill the tank, but she never approaches the pump, and in twenty minutes her parents are back with large paper coffee cups. Will moves in a little closer.

'I hear your fiancé might join us for a few days,' says Genevieve.

'Yes, Mother. If he can get away.'

'We're naming the new hospital addition the Claudine du Lac Wing. You should be proud to have your name associated with such a worthy project.'

'You can't imagine,' she says, checking her lipstick and returning the small mirror to her pocket.

'Would you ladies get the lead out?' says Jean-Rene, climbing in the pilot's seat. He checks the instrument panel and taps the fuel gauge, then taps it again. 'There's not even a quarter tank here!' he says.

'The gauge is sticky, Daddy. I topped

off the tank but it didn't register on the dial.'

'I have no time for this right now. Remind me to get it fixed as soon as we get back.'

'I won't forget,' she says. She and Genevieve move arm and arm toward the plane. Claudine suddenly doubles over, holding her lower abdomen, her knees sinking to the tarmac.

'What is it?' says her mother.

'I'm going to be sick,' says Claudine. 'It's my appendix again.'

Jean-Rene jumps down from the plane. 'Oh for god's sake!' he says. 'I'm supposed to meet a realtor about a piece of land in two hours. Are you sure you couldn't find a more inconvenient moment to have the vapors?'

Will comes out from the hangar and strides over. 'Maybe I can help, sir,' he says. 'I'll take her straight to the E.R. so you can continue with your plans.'

'I know you,' says Jean-Rene. 'You're the fellow with that classic Apache. Braxton, isn't it?'

'Bratton. Will Bratton, sir.'

'Of course.'

'Please Daddy, you and Mother go on ahead. I'll call the lodge this evening and let you know what Dr. O'Grady says.'

'It's your funeral, kid.' He turns to Genevieve. 'Get in the plane.'

'I don't know. Maybe I should — '

'Now!' says the voice of authority.

Claudine maintains the mask of innocent suffering as her mother boards the flight. As soon as the plane rises into a porcelain-blue sky, she shoves Wilbur away. 'You've got a nerve putting your dirty hands on me,' she says. 'I should call security.'

'I was thinking of calling them myself,' he says with a crooked smile.

There's a telling pause. 'How long have you been spying on me?'

'Long enough,' he says with self-assured calmness.

'What the hell is that supposed to mean?' Claudine is suddenly transformed from a purring little kitten to a box of tiger claws.

'I topped off the tank, daddy dear, but it didn't register,' he mimics.

The color drains from her face and she

almost passes out. This time it's for real.

'On a quarter tank they should come down in the middle of the Lac du Flambeau Indian Reservation. What do you think?'

She begins to tremble all over.

'Come on, you need a drink,' he says, offering a supportive arm. 'We have business to discuss.'

★   ★   ★

She was 21 that day. She wore a fluttery summer dress and looked like she belonged on the cover of *Seventeen Magazine*. Today she's 27 and looks like Playmate of the Year. Will was 42 back then. Today he feels 80.

It takes twenty minutes to drain the fuel tank and replace just enough to keep the plane in the air for half an hour. He hears a car start at the bottom of the hill, but the vehicle is blocked from view by a stand of trees. He sets the heavy fuel containers along the back wall of the hangar. When he reaches the bottom of the hill, Marlis Underhill's car is gone.

11

Deep Chill

It's late and I can't sleep. I stand in the moonlight by the window looking out at the town square. I'm restless and wired on coffee.

'Aren't you coming to bed?' says Frack. I turn from the window and sit on the edge of the bed. He takes my hand. 'What is it, Robely?'

'I think Will Bratton is on the verge of talking.'

'About the heist?'

'About Claudine. His marriage hasn't met his expectations.'

I see the amusement in Frack's eyes. 'That makes him part of a very big club.'

'Remember when I read the column about Claudine dumping her fiancé to marry Will?' I say.

'Yes. Why?'

'Michael Anderson dumped *her*.'

'That's very interesting.'

'He told me the people closest to her have uncharacteristically bad luck. When her sister drowned, she profited. When her parents died, she became richer than Midas. When Albert Paxton died, a potential lawsuit disappeared. I'd call that a pattern.'

'And Ruth?'

'She knew too much.'

'We won't know for certain what killed Al until after the post-mortem,' says Frack. 'Besides, why poison a man if he's already dying of Crohn's?'

'He wasn't dying fast enough. Will was only days from meeting with Al's lawyer.'

'That gives both Claudine and Will a motive.'

The phone rings. Marlis's caller I.D. comes up on the screen. It's 2:45 a.m. 'Marlis?' I say.

'No. It's Rosalie. I'm worried. Marlis said she'd be back around eleven thirty and she's not home yet.'

'Have you called the chateau?'

'No one picks up.'

'I'm driving out there. Call my cell if

she makes it home in the meantime.' I click off. 'That was Rosalie Dearborn. Marlis went to the chateau for dinner and she's not back yet. I'm going to drive out there.'

Frack gets out of bed and pulls on his warm clothes. 'Please, stay in bed and get some sleep.'

'Not on your life,' I say.

★ ★ ★

The moment Wilbur sneaks back into the hospital, he's confronted by an angry nurse.

'Where were you, Mr. Bratton? We were about to report you missing.'

'I went for a smoke. There's not one ashtray in this joint.'

'I want you gowned up and back in bed. The phlebotomist is coming. The doctor wants to check your white count. If you don't behave, I'll shackle you to the bars.'

Once Wilbur is settled, the needle man, who looks like Mickey Rourke in *The Wrestler*, takes a syringe and digs around in his arm until he locates a vein.

'Why don't you use a pitchfork?' growls
Will.

'You're one of the lucky ones. You
should see me on a bad day.'

★　★　★

Frack drives slowly toward Little Papoose
Lake as I sweep the riverbank with my
flashlight. There's no indication that
Marlis has gone off the road. When we
pull up to the chateau, the windows are
dark. A horse whinnies softly from the
stable.

Parked in front of the house is a black
late-model pickup and a silver sports
car, but no sign of Marlis's vehicle. I
shine my light on the damaged front end
of the truck and shoot Frack a knowing
glance.

I ring the doorbell. It's several minutes
before Claudine snaps on the porch light
and opens the door. Her hair is in
disarray. She looks like she's been
sleeping in her street clothes.

'Mrs. Bratton?' I say.

'Do you have any idea what time it is?' she says.

'Three fifteen. You're up late.'

'I fell asleep on the couch. Can't this wait until morning?'

'You show an amazing lack of curiosity for someone whose husband is lying in the hospital,' says Frack. 'Most people would wonder why two deputies are standing on their porch.'

'Why don't you enlighten me?'

'I understand Miss Underhill was here this evening.'

'That's right. We had dinner together.'

'When did she leave?'

'Around ten thirty or eleven.'

'She hasn't returned home,' I say. 'Her roommate is worried.'

'I guess she stopped off somewhere. A bar. A boyfriend's place. You're the detectives.'

'May we come in? It's bone-chilling out here,' I say.

'I'm going to bed.' She starts to close the door, but I stick my foot in the opening and smile nicely.

'You've got to be kidding,' she says. 'I

thought they only did that in the movies.'

'Just one more question. How did you damage the front end of your pickup?'

'My gardener picked up a load of planting soil and hit a stop sign.'

'What's his name?'

'Jose. No. Ramon. What difference does it make? He's already gone back to Mexico.'

She closes the door and turns off the porch light before we reach our car.

*   *   *

Marlis slowly regains consciousness. It takes several seconds to collect her thoughts and get them in proper order. It's cold. Her scalp is sticky with blood but the bleeding has subsided. Her head throbs as she pulls herself to a sitting position.

Through a small vent near the ceiling she hears the crunch of gravel as a car pulls up to the house. After a few minutes it leaves.

She makes her way to the top of the stairs. The door is locked. She presses her ear to the wood, but hears nothing. She goes back down, leaning against the wall for support. The cellar is quiet except for the electric hum of freezers. She explores her surroundings, her lungs adjusting little by little to the cold. If only she hadn't picked up those damn keys, she'd be back at Lovelace House. Now she wonders if she'll make it out of here alive.

Curious, she opens a freezer. It's loaded with TV dinners and ice cream. Another contains packages of wild game. She opens the last one. Inside is the diminutive body of Ruth Chambers. Her eyes are open. There's frozen blood and broken glass in her hair. Alive when she was imprisoned here, her palms are lifted in a dying effort to push up the lid of her tomb.

Marlis closes the freezer and continues to explore her surroundings. She sees no means of escape but finds items that could prove useful: flashlight, fire extinguisher, ice pick, screwdriver, hand ax. She's not so naive as to think Claudine intends to let her live.

She climbs the stairs with the ice pick, screwdriver and hand ax, inserts the tips of the pick and screwdriver into the keyhole and uses the side of the ax to pound them screeching into the hole. *Try to get your key in there, Ms. Du Lac.*

Back downstairs she notices two metal boxes screwed into a floor-to-ceiling wooden post. One is the electrical box. A telephone cable sprouts from the other. Her first thought is to flip the main breaker, but why be so delicate?

Instead she takes the ax and smashes both boxes into scrap metal. There's a flash and a shower of sparks and the light goes out on the ceiling. The freezers go silent. If she dies here, she's going to leave one hell of a calling card in blood and wreckage. Let Claudine explain *this*! She sits down at the end of the wine rack and waits.

★ ★ ★

'We need a search warrant,' I say as we drive back toward town.

'Suspicion is not the same as probable

cause,' says Frack. 'Judge Adams will never go for it.'

'I need access to that house.'

'You *want* access to that house.'

'Marlis never made it out of there.'

'Then where's her car?'

'I don't know.'

'What if she stopped at an all-night grocery store? When she comes home with a loaf of bread we're going to look pretty silly.'

'There isn't an all-night grocery for thirty miles.'

'I wasn't being literal. I'm trying to make a point.'

'I want to go back in the daylight. You can't see a damn thing out there at night.'

'The same rules apply. If we're asked to leave, we have to go.' Pale moonlight slides across the hood of the car. Ice breaking up on the river sounds like rifle shots.

'Want to hear *my* idea?' asks Frack.

'Of course.'

'Let's talk to Will Bratton.'

'Why?'

'If he gives us permission to enter the

chateau, we don't need Claudine or Judge Adams. It only takes the consent of one adult resident for law enforcement to make legal entry.'

'Frack, my love, you are a genius.'

★ ★ ★

Claudine hears a fearful clatter coming from the bowels of the house. Marlis Underhill is alive! She runs upstairs, grabs her Luger along with the iron key, and runs back downstairs to get the job done right.

Ruth had been far less trouble. At 98 lbs., she'd simply lifted the unconscious woman into the freezer and latched the lid. But Marlis is too statuesque to be lifted by one woman — at least in one piece. She briefly considers saws and knives but doesn't have the stomach for it.

The racket from the cellar continues until she's halfway across the living room and the house goes dark. A thick silence ensues. She trips over a lamp cord reaching for the switch. A fern frond, feeling every bit like spider legs, brushes across her face. She screams and knocks the pot from its pedestal, scattering soil and pottery shards across the floor. She tries the wall switch, but it too is dead. She pulls open the drapes and lets in the first thin light of dawn.

She knows the deputies will be back, probably with search warrants. Of course, they'll want access to the cellar. Before they come she'll finish off Marlis, drag her behind a storage crate and wash the blood down the cellar drain. But that still leaves the problem of Ruth. Faced with growing complications, she breaks into a cold, trembling sweat. There's too much to do and no time to get it done.

She must collect herself. She is, after all, a du Lac. They do not crumble under stress.

She approaches the cellar door and sees strange projectiles sticking from the keyhole, the business end of a screwdriver and the point of an ice pick. She gets a hammer from a kitchen drawer and tries to drive the instruments back through the hole so she can insert her key. She only succeeds in pounding them into a tangle. That's when the wine bottles start smashing against the other side of the door. One, two. She stops counting at twenty. There's more to Marlis Underhill than a beautiful face and long division.

⋆   ⋆   ⋆

The sun rises as Frack and I head toward the hospital. The phone rings. It's Paula. I put her on speaker.

'Guess who I have on my autopsy table?'

'Albert Paxton,' I say.

'Yes. Judge Adams jumped on it. He called in a forensic toxicologist from the university to assist in the autopsy. I'll touch bases later. His car is just pulling in.'

When Frack and I arrive at the hospital, Will is being discharged.

'I was hoping for a clean getaway,' he says with his usual gruff humor.

'Marlis is missing. We think she's at the chateau,' I say.

Will opens his mouth but clamps it

shut again. 'So what do you want from me?'

'Access to the house.'

Since he'd heard her drive away last night, he knows they won't find her there. 'Sure, why not.'

'Into the wheelchair, Mr. Bratton,' says the nurse.

'Do I look like an invalid?'

'I'm sure you could swim with polar bears, but — '

'I know. Hospital policy.'

★   ★   ★

Claudine races to her bedroom and grabs her passport. She spills pounds of Krugerrands, expensive jewelry and stacks of banded paper money from a wall safe into her overnight case. She loves Chateau du Lac, but she loves freedom more.

She stuffs two large suitcases until the seams are about to pop. From the upstairs window she sees the gardener arrive and throws the window open. 'Romero,' she calls. 'Come to my room.'

'*Sí*, Señora Claudine.' He's gorgeous, just out of high school, hotter than a pistol between the sheets.

'It's something else this morning,' she says when he comes in. 'A sudden emergency.'

He smiles to cover his disappointment at the change of plan. 'When I get back,' she says, softly kissing his lips. 'Here, take this.' She presses a stack of bills in his hand. 'Now, you must hurry. Load my bags into the Apache. If anyone asks, tell them I'll be back tomorrow.'

When the plane is loaded and ready, Claudine climbs into the cockpit. From her vantage point on the runway she sees Will's Caddy leading a cop car onto Lakeside Drive. She's no Amelia Earhart, but she can get a plane in the sky and land it on a dime. Within hours she'll be in Canada, then onto a commercial flight to some distant paradise where the natives have no word for snow and she can lounge like a cat in the sun. Flowers will tumble over sunny stucco walls, fountains will splash on adobe stones, help will be cheap and lovers young and eager.

The dual propellers whir — a heavenly sound like angel's wings. One thing about Will, he keeps a well-maintained machine. As she taxis down the runway, the cars pull up to the house, lights flashing. The plane rises into a porcelain-blue sky, so like that long-ago day when she pulled off the biggest score of her life.

She banks sharply to the left and the cumbersome luggage shifts with a thud. The plane tilts toward the left wing and she can't straighten it out. There's a drop in momentum, an ominous shudder, and the plane is no longer rising. In fact, she's losing altitude at an alarming rate. From the ground, Will and the deputies watch the red and white Apache roll wing over wing, writing Claudine's destiny against the sky like a graceful bird.

In a mindless panic, Claudine looks toward the passenger seat and sees her father smiling at her. 'What's happening?'

'You're doing just fine, baby,' he says.

'Daddy, help me! We're going down.'

'I've gone down before. It's not that bad.'

'You're not listening.'

'Mom's waiting for us at the other end. Patrice too. Can you believe she hasn't aged a day in all these years?' Jean-Rene casually lights his pipe. 'I missed out on that real estate deal, you know. A real shame.' He rests his head against the back of the seat, the sunlight warm on his face. 'Not a cloud in sight,' he says. 'You couldn't have picked a lovelier day for a flight.'

As the people on the ground scan the sky, a huge gold fireball blossoms above the treeline a mile or two from the chateau.

'Holy Christ!' says Frack.

'Mother of god!' says Romero, dropping to his knees. He presses a rosary to lips still warm from Claudine's kiss.

* * *

I follow Marlis's voice down a long corridor to the cellar door. Strange implements poke like silver porcupine quills out of the keyhole.

'Marlis, it's Robely. Frack is with me.'

'Get me out. I'm freezing to death.'

Within fifteen minutes the property is teeming with law enforcement from every surrounding locale. The first fire unit goes directly to the site of the crash. A firefighter from the second truck takes an ax and turns the ancient door into toothpicks. Medics whisk Marlis to the ambulance. I squeeze her hand as she's loaded inside and carried off.

When I return to the house, Frack is coming up from the cellar. 'Ruth is no longer a missing person,' he says. 'She's in the freezer. Mike is on the phone to the coroner's office.'

'Finding Ruth will hopefully give Phyllis and Violet some sense of closure.'

We go upstairs to Claudine's bedroom. There are clothes and shoes thrown everywhere, and the wall safe is empty. I look in the jewelry box and find a small bottle filled with a heavy liquid.

'Don't touch it,' says Frack. 'It's ethylene glycol. The more I learn, the less I believe that Will had anything to do with Al's death.'

'You may be right. Claudine probably poisoned the drink she took from Will's hand before she gave it to Al the night of the party.'

'But Will had to have known that Claudine was responsible for her parents' death. If nothing else, he's an accessory after the fact.'

'We'll never prove it. There's too much water gone under the bridge.'

We walk outside and look around. Mike has vanished. Two state police cars pull up and four troopers get out.

'Everyone wants a piece of this case,' says Frack. 'It has everything: a mansion, a sexy blonde, a few homicides.'

Mike emerges from the bridle path that runs along the river. He walks up to us, wet to his waist. 'I'm calling for a dive team,' he says. 'Two cars are submerged in the lake.'

'Two?' says Frack.

'A green Chevy just off shore and another car about twenty feet out. One belongs to Marlis Underhill. The other is probably Ruth Chambers's.'

Will Bratton comes puffing down the hill covered in ash and smelling of diesel fuel.

'Do not light that cigar or you'll go up like a Roman candle,' I say.

'Geez, I didn't know you cared.'

'I care when you're standing two feet away. My concern diminishes with distance,' I say. 'Any idea what went wrong with the plane?'

'She was overloaded and the cargo shifted. That plane was my pride and joy.'

'And Claudine?' says Mike.

'Let's just say cremation would be redundant. She just saved you a lot of work and the state a lot of money.'

Big Mike studies my face. I know what he's thinking. I smile and try to look bright-eyed. 'When is the last time you got any sleep?' he asks me.

'I'm fine,' I say.

'Two nights ago,' says Frack.

'Sheriff Brooker is on his way,' says Mike. 'We're taking over from here. You two go home and get some rest. Take tomorrow off. Take two.'

I open my mouth.

'Go!' he says.

★　★　★

Frack and I sleep until the next afternoon when Paula calls.

'We've got what we need, Robely. Ruth Chambers was right — Al's kidneys are full of crystals. Curiosity cost an intelligent woman her life, but with Claudine gone we have no one to prosecute. The only thing left is putting the paperwork in order.'

'I wonder what Will Bratton will do with all those millions?' I ask.

'Whatever it is, he'll probably be filing bankruptcy in seven years,' says Paula with a laugh. 'Turns out Burgess Bratton's night-stick matches the wound on Harry Joe Madden's throat, so he won't be going anywhere for a while. Ever find out who sold the coat to Baby Boy Clemson?'

'Maybe Hank Logan. Burgess wouldn't have offed it this close to home.'

'Did you hear that Clemson's rival, Big Roller, was found dead from a stab wound a couple blocks from The Franklin?'

'Never heard of him.'

'He had a healing bullet wound in his leg. He could be the guy you winged that night. Miss Cream Puff used to be a part of his stable until she went off with Clemson.'

'Sounds like a motive to me. We have to clean up that place one of these days, but I'm too tired to think about it now.'

'Later, kid. Get some rest.'

I call the hospital. Marlis is back home after being treated for hypothermia and receiving six staples in her scalp.

'This is our day off, remember?' says Frack, patting the bed beside him.

★   ★   ★

'I'll miss you,' says Luisa, giving Sylvia a big hug. 'I'm sorry about the way things worked out.'

'I had a great time. We'll get together in July and take your mother on a boat tour of the Chain O' Lakes.'

'*What?*'

'April Fools!'

'You had me going there. Give my best to Rosalie. Now that you're with Kent, don't throw her overboard without a life jacket.'

Sylvia drives leisurely toward home. At dinnertime she stops at a café for a club sandwich.

There's a display case of silver jewelry beside the cash register. A dainty pair of unicorn earrings catches her eye. They match Rosalie's tattoo. Sylvia buys them as a peace offering. Thirty miles out of Abundance, a bank of storm clouds sweeps in from the west.

*   *   *

Rosalie parks around the side of the building and steps unsteadily into the rain. She finishes off a fifth of Southern Comfort and lets the bottle fall to the asphalt. When Kent sees her approaching, he whisks her inside and swings her in a circle.

'God, am I glad to see you,' he says. 'I thought I'd have to wait until the third.'

'I couldn't stay away another minute.'

'Are you hungry?'

'Just cold.'

'Let's go upstairs where it's warm,' he says. She follows him, careful not to weave or stumble. 'I didn't see your car.'

'There was broken glass out front so I parked around the side.'

He takes her coat and hangs it up. There's a flash of lightning. Thunder rolls across the roof. 'Let me look at you,' he says, his eyes shining. Her beauty takes his breath away. Her soft black hair invites his touch. Her cheekbones are more pronounced than he remembers, her profile more defined. 'You've lost weight.'

'I had a cold, but I'm better now.'

'Lie back on the bed. Let me help you out of those wet shoes.'

She floats like a lily on a lake as he removes her shoes and sets them by the radiator to dry. 'Anything else you want to remove?' she says.

'Right now?'

'There's no time like the present,' she says.

★ ★ ★

Stolen love, borrowed love intended for someone else — but she'll take it. Once it's done, no one can ever take it back or undo it, or pretend it never happened.

Something changes, like when a door opens and a cold draft sucks the heat from the room. It's as if he's snapped out of a trance. 'What is this?' he says, shoving her away. 'Some sick game?'

'What's wrong?'

His eyes are locked on her right shoulder. 'Sylvia's tattoo is a butterfly, not a unicorn.' He forcefully, fearfully throws her off the bed. She lands in a heap, her head hitting the closet door with a bang. Car headlights sweep across the ceiling. 'Who the hell are you?' he says, pulling on his jeans.

'I — I — It's a joke. Just an April Fool's joke.' She gets to her feet and pulls on her coat, leaving the rest of her things behind. She stumbles down the staircase and bumps into Sylvia, who looks at her in stunned disbelief.

Rosalie makes a strange animal sound, half laugh, half moan. Sylvia pushes her aside and races up the stairs to the apartment where Rosalie's underthings lay scattered about.

'Wait. I can explain,' says Kent. 'Please,

give me just one minute.' But Sylvia is already gone.

Rosalie has a head start but it won't last long. Her twin has the newer, faster car, and she has no idea what Sylvia will do when she catches up. She swings onto an unpaved road that twists through the farmland. A couple more detours and Sylvia is still behind her and gaining. Three miles from town she passes her, flying toward home.

Rosalie asks herself what she would do if she were Sylvia. It would have to be a definitive statement — clothes doused with bleach; Crazy Glue squirted in dancing shoes; jewelry flushed down the toilet.

She rounds a curve and sees Sylvia standing on the side of the road, her hair dripping with rain, her car on its side in the ditch. Rosalie is giddy with relief. Her sister might catch up to her, but not tonight.

12

Up in Flames

'Get up!' screams Rosalie. 'The house is on fire.'

Marlis sits up, her airway constricted from the smoke, still weak from loss of blood and sore from the staples in her scalp. She throws on her robe and runs to the door.

'We can't get out that way,' says Rosalie. 'We can't get out of the window either, not with those damn boards.'

'Call nine-one-one,' says Marlis, grabbing a hammer from the closet. 'I'll work on the boards and we'll climb down the tree.'

Rosalie opens her phone, but her voice falls into a hole of nothingness. 'It's dead.'

'Then help me.'

The nails squeal as they pry the first board two inches from the wall. 'Watch out.' Marlis whacks it with the hammer and it rattles to the floor. 'Don't step on the nails,' she says.

They knock off one more board, but there still isn't enough room to squeeze through. They press their faces to the opening and pull fresh air into their lungs. Tree branches scrape against the siding, rain surfing across the slate roof.

They scream for help but no one hears them. From the attic, the ground seems miles and miles below. *'Help! Help! Fire!'* Their words spin away on the wind. A light snaps on in the trailer park at the end of No Name Road. 'I think someone heard us,' says Marlis. They scream until their throats are raw.

'We're wasting time,' says Rosalie. The fire has eaten through the door, the room thick with smoke. The influx of oxygen only feeds the fire.

Marlis attacks the next board. Her face has gone grey and the inhaler she so desperately needs is in her coat pocket back at the chateau. She struggles for air and sinks to her knees as flames crawl up the wallpaper. The bulb in the ceiling fixture explodes.

'Get up, goddamn it!' screams Rosalie, pulling her roommate up by the hair. A staple in Marlis's scalp rips loose and she yelps in pain. She tries to stay on her feet but sinks to the floor again, her fingernails and lips a ghostly cyanotic blue.

Rosalie leaves Marlis where she's fallen. If she's going to save someone's skin, it's going to be her own. The intense heat chases her into the kitchenette. Her nostrils clog with ash. Her eyes clamp shut. She fumbles for a dish towel, moistens it beneath the faucet, and breathes through it. The floor beneath her feet is hot as fire devours the timbers of the second-floor ceiling. She hears barking, distant and frenzied. Miss Jennie. Woofie. She can't think about that now. She tips over a cookie jar on the counter, topples the blender. Her fingers touch the dishwasher, then the refrigerator . . .

The refrigerator. *The refrigerator!*

She throws open the door and sweeps the contents to the floor, sending shelves clattering across the room, all the time slapping sparks from her pajamas. The smoke is too dense to see Marlis drag herself to her feet and resume her feeble assault on the boards.

Rosalie chokes in a breath and crawls into the porcelain cave. She pulls the door shut and thinks of Sylvia breathing cool rain-washed air. With knees drawn to her chin, she waits in suffocating darkness like a mummy in a tomb. She wants to tell Sylvia she's sorry. Her sister will never know she died with those words stuck in her throat.

* * *

The ache in Tex's bad hip keeps him awake. Still dressed, he goes to the kitchen. He's filling the tea kettle when he looks out the window and sees flames behind the windows of Lovelace House.

He drops the kettle in the sink. 'Oh my god!' He grabs a fire extinguisher from the broom closet and pounds on the door of his neighbor's trailer. 'Lovelace House is on fire!'

His neighbor, Grady Tyner, throws a robe over his pajamas. His wife Astrid calls 911. 'The closest fire engine is fourteen miles away,' she says. 'They're suiting up now.'

Fourteen miles! It might as well be one hundred. Tex power-limps down No Name Road with Grady beside him. Word has spread fast, and a swelling tide of people surges toward the burning house.

'Look,' says Grady, pointing to the attic. 'A woman is leaning out of the window. It's the one with the long red hair.'

★ ★ ★

Even the warm, rolling ocean of the waterbed can't lull Kent to sleep. Sylvia may not have had a jealous husband with a gun, but she'd somehow forgotten to mention the nymphomaniac twin with a few screws loose.

Unable to sleep, he turns on the tube. A TV announcer stands in a crowd outside a burning house. '*Fire is ripping through the historic Lovelace House in Abundance. The four residents of the home have not been seen since the blaze began.*'

Kent jumps up and grabs his phone. He dials Sylvia's cell.

'What?' she says despondently.

'Please, don't hang up. Where are you?'

'My car's in a ditch near Shepard's Farm.'

'Thank god! I'm coming to get you. Lovelace House is on fire.'

★　★　★

Grady Tyner goes straight for the oak tree. In his fifties and out of shape, he still monkeys up the broad slippery branches, rain flattening what little hair is left on his head. Astrid grabs the garden hose, but it's frozen as stiff as a rake handle.

Tex has to get inside, but the back entrance is fitted with a locked security door. He rushes out front and climbs onto the veranda. He sends the fire extinguisher crashing through the glass oval, reaches inside and releases the lock. He enters the hall, black with smoke. He sees no fire and tosses the extinguisher aside.

'Jennie!' he calls. 'Jennie!'

No answer. He hears the dog barking and follows the sound. He feels his way along the wall and opens the bedroom door. He finds Miss Jennie on the floor beside the bed. The dog bolts past him to freedom. Tex's bad hip gives an ominous pop as he lifts her into his arms. He limps his way outside and across the street, where Grady is sitting on a neighbor's step comforting Marlis as she struggles to breathe.

Tex gives Jennie a series of chest compressions until he hears a dry cough and she opens her eyes. 'The girls?' she says.

'Marlis is out. I don't know about the others.'

'Woofie?'

'He's okay. Hiding under a house somewhere.'

'Mr. Holzheimer?'

'I thought he was too ornery to die, but he didn't make it.'

A pickup pulls up to the curb. Sylvia Dearborn and Kent jump to the ground. Behind them is the fire truck. By the time they hook up to the hydrant, two ambulances have arrived.

'Where's Rosalie?' says Sylvia, her voice breaking. Before she gets a response, there's a loud cracking of beams. Several onlookers gasp and run further from the inferno. Flames and sparks shower skyward as the house collapses downward with a roar.

'Oh my god! Rosalie's in there,' Sylvia cries, grabbing Kent's arm.

The firemen blast the burning rubble with their hoses and spray down the roof of the carriage house. Sparks fly as a soot-coated refrigerator tumbles end over end from a great height. It hits hard and pops open on impact.

'Holy mother of god!' shouts one of the firemen. 'There's a person in there.'

Sylvia screams. 'That's my sister!'

Kent runs across the street and climbs over the rubble.

'No!' shouts the fire chief, but Kent keeps going. The heavy soles of his boots smoke and start melting. His jacket and pants cuffs catch fire. 'Get the hose on him,' the chief calls out. The captain turns down the velocity of the water so he doesn't blow the kid into the center of the flames. He drenches him along with the surrounding area, giving Kent the time he needs to lift the wet, limp body of Rosalie Dearborn from her tomb. He rushes her to the sidewalk across the street, where medics put an oxygen mask over her face and begin CPR. It seems a hopeless effort, but they get a weak, uneven pulse. A second team gives Marlis oral cortico-steroids and her color improves.

Marlis and Miss Jennie, accompanied by Tex, are transported to the hospital. Rosalie, accompanied by Sylvia and Kent, follow in a second. Whether its final destination is the hospital or the morgue is anyone's guess.

★   ★   ★

It's past midnight, but Sheriff Brooker, Mike, Frack, Paula and I still sit in the city hall office of District Attorney Jay Cranston, presenting our evidence against Burgess Bratton in the murder of Harry Joe Madden during the commission of a felony. He will also face charges in the attempted murder of his brother Will Bratton.

'A cop? He'll get a cozy welcome in the penitentiary,' says Cranston.

With the discovery of Ruth Chambers's body and the bottle of antifreeze in Claudine's bedroom, both inquiries come to an end. As ex-fiancé Michael Anderson said: 'The people closest to Claudine have uncharacteristically bad luck.' As it turned out, so did she.

No charges are leveled against Will. The servants swear he was never allowed access to the iron key or permitted in the cellar; it was Claudine's exclusive domain. That doesn't mean he hadn't blackmailed Claudine into marriage, but I don't care. Their retribution came in the form of one another.

As we conclude our meeting, my cell phone vibrates. It's Gladys. Frack and I are exhausted. Should I or shouldn't I?

'Yes, Mom.'

'Honey, Lovelace House has burned to the ground. The whole western sky is still glowing.'

'Oh my god! Did everyone make it out?'

'I don't know. They've got the street cordoned off.'

By the time we arrive at Euclid, the firemen are hosing down the last of the flames. They allow us to cross the barrier. The heat is still intense, and all that remains of the once-historic property is a pile of smoking rubble and a carriage house.

'Did they make it out?' Frack asks one of the firemen.

'Two came out alive. The medics were trying to revive a third during transport.'

'What about the fourth?' I ask.

'What fourth?'

★   ★   ★

A week after the fire, Rosalie regains consciousness. Sylvia and Cousin Luisa are at her bedside. She asks the usual questions of someone coming out of a coma. 'Where am I? What happened?' Then as memory returns, 'Did everyone make it out?'

'Everyone else has been treated and released back to their somewhat altered lives,' says Sylvia. 'You've suffered a lot of smoke inhalation. It will take time before you're back up to speed. Marlis has rented office space in Promontory with living quarters above. Miss Jennie and Woofie will be staying with her, at least for now. Tex got Jennie out of the fire and a man from No Name Road got Marlis out.'

'I deserve what's happened to me,' says Rosalie. 'Del was right. I *am* the bad twin.'

'That's nonsense. Leaving me stranded saved me from the fire.'

'My life is one disaster after another. Del is gone. Mom won't speak to me. My life ended that night at the bridge.'

'You had nothing to do with your father's leaving,' says Luisa. 'You provided a convenient excuse so he could shack up with that barmaid he'd been seeing.'

'And let's face it,' says Sylvia, 'Mom is about as easy to live with as Aunt Cecile.'

'We're all in agreement on that one,' says Luisa, snorting a laugh.

'I can't imagine Lovelace House being

gone,' says Rosalie. 'Now I have no place to go home to.'

'Sylvia and I have been talking about that. How about the inn? You can recuperate and stay as long as you like. Maybe you can help me find a husband.'

'Thank you. That sounds like fun.'

'How would you like to be my maid of honor?' says Sylvia.

'Kent hates me!'

'He doesn't hate you. We can have the ceremony right here. You don't even have to get out of bed.'

'Okay, I'll do it. You never said who pulled me out of the fire.'

'Your future brother-in-law. Be nice or he'll throw you back.'

★ ★ ★

Marlis, Miss Jennie and Woofie stand on the sidewalk looking at the charred remains of Lovelace House. 'Have you heard anything from Will Bratton lately?' asks Jennie.

'Now that he has money, he's come clean with the IRS. I've never been so happy to be off the hook.'

'I bet.'

'He wants to buy another plane and give flying lessons.'

Jennie laughs so hard tears spring to her eyes. 'With that family history? I don't know if he can find enough suicide hopefuls to keep him in business.'

'He's bulldozed the storage lot; sold it to a farmer who wants to grow corn.'

'Wisconsin needs more corn like Arizona needs more cactus.'

'What about the employees?'

'Hank and Benny? Claudine left them each a modest monthly stipend in perpetuity.'

Jennie looks over at the pile of rubble. 'I was born here and I thought I'd die here. Now I'm as poor as a church mouse. The people on No Name Road sure have the last laugh on me.'

'Look,' says Marlis. 'We have company.'

Jennie turns to see a well-dressed man getting out of his car with a camera and clipboard. 'Oh god, another gawker,' she says as he walks up to them. 'You in the market for a pile of nicely charred wood?'

she asks. 'All you have to do is haul it off.'

'Are you Jennie Lee Lovelace?'

'Who wants to know?'

'I'm Jonathan Hull from Farmer's Insurance. We carry the policy on your house.'

'What policy? You haven't billed me in a year and I haven't paid you a dime.'

'Miss Lovelace, over a year ago you gave signed authorization to change your billing to automatic withdrawal. Don't you remember?'

'Not really.'

'That's why you haven't been able to balance your checkbook,' says Marlis.

Jennie gives the man a skeptical look. 'You mean you're going to build me a new house?'

'Yes. That's why I'm here,' he says.

It takes a moment to sink in. Her energy comes back in a rush. 'I want a different floor plan — a sprawling one-story, like the Sinatra house in Palm Springs. I'm tired of living in the musty old past.'

'The lady certainly knows what she wants,' says Hull.

'Besides, I'm too old to climb all those stairs. And once the carpets are in, I want the workmen to wipe their feet on the mat before they step inside.'

'We'll discuss all of your concerns. I promise.' He takes out his pen. 'Do you know how the fire started? The fire chief thinks it began on the second floor.'

She pauses to reflect on the leaky chimney and the brick that fell onto the grate. 'I have no idea,' she says.

'Well, let me look around.'

'Here comes Tex,' says Marlis. He parks at the curb and limps over. She introduces him to Mr. Hull.

Marlis looks at her wristwatch. 'I have a lunch date with Mark in half an hour.'

'You go ahead,' says Tex. 'I'll drive Jennie back when she's ready.'

'You want me to take Woofie with me?' she says.

'Please, dear. He gets bored just standing around.'

Tex turns to Jennie and Mr. Hull.

'When you're through here, how about we go to my place and you two can brainstorm over a cup of coffee.'

'That's a very agreeable offer,' says Mr. Hull.

13

Spring

The man in the uniform whistles Fargo up the basement stairs to the warm kitchen. He's starving and goes straight for a bowl of cat food sitting beside the stove. The woman snatches it away and sets it on the counter.

'I'll warm up the car,' says the man.

Fargo turns from the crabby-faced woman and dances in circles, his toenails clicking on the linoleum. He knows the word *car*. It's one of his favorite words along with *french fries*, *walk-in-the-woods* and *Raggedy Ann*. Is he finally going home?

When the man returns from the garage, the woman shoves a deer rifle at him. 'Take him into the woods,' she says.

'Is this really necessary?'

'If Burgess talks, your name is bound to come up.'

'So what? You act like I murdered someone, Eleanor. All I've done is hide a dog for Crissake!'

'We need to break any connection between us, the chief and those two deputies.' The woman's eyes are hard as stone. The man takes the gun.

'Come on, Fuzzball,' he says. 'We're going for a ride.'

* * *

I'm sitting in front of the fireplace in my pink pajamas and slippers, mellowed out on orange brandy and listening to rain tap on the window. Frack is still dressed in his black jogging suit, absorbed in Michael Connelly's latest mystery novel.

'I can't believe all of our cases have been resolved,' I say. 'Claudine is dead. Burgess is behind bars. Ruth Chambers has received a proper Christian burial, and Elan will get most of their furs back. David Coburn is even starting to regain his memory.'

'Yup, we did good, kid,' says Frack, setting the book aside.

'Have you noticed that when it warms up the rain sounds softer against the window?'

'No, I hadn't noticed that. Did you know that Sheriff Brooker wants to give an award dinner in your honor?'

'You're joking, right?'

'Nope.'

'For what? Getting myself shot?'

'I think it's for your investigative expertise.'

'Oh, bunk! He's a publicity hound. He wants his picture in the paper handing me a ribbon. You have to talk him out of it, Frack.'

'Why?'

I walk over and sit on his lap. 'You know I have trouble speaking in formal settings. Besides, I'd have to buy a dress that I'd probably never wear again. If he presses the issue, I'll sprain my ankle to get out of it, just like Big Mike would.'

'I'll see what I can do.'

'Thank you.'

He buries his face in my hair. 'God, you smell good.'

'It's coconut shampoo from the Dollar

Store. Two bottles for a buck.'

'On you it smells like a million bucks.'

The phone vibrates beneath the chair cushion. Frack pulls it out and answers. 'For you,' he says. 'It's you-know-who.'

'I'm going to kill you,' I mouth. 'Hi, Mom. What's up?'

'I need you down at the bar, honey. A drunk has passed out on the floor.'

'Mom, I'm in my pajamas. Call him a cab.'

'Last time he threw up on the seat. They won't take him anymore. He's polished off a whole bucket in the last half hour.' I hear the patrons snickering in the background.

I roll my eyes. I look cross-eyed at the phone. 'Okay, fill me in. How much does he weigh?'

'He used to be about 120, but now he's down to 100.'

'He doesn't sound very formidable. You've handled drunks three times that size.' No response. 'Is he prone to violence?'

'He's never bitten anyone that I know of.'

There's a full beat of dead silence before I start screaming. I jump off Frack's lap. I run down the stairs and out of the house. I hear him telling me to wait, that he'll get the car, that I need my coat, but I keep on running down the sidewalk toward the Little Papoose River. Someone opens a window along my route.

'It's that lady cop,' says a female voice. 'She's running through the rain in her pajamas.'

'Any woman who'd take on that job has to be a little nuts,' says her husband.

Frack catches up to me. I jump in the car and put on my raincoat. I try to explain, except I'm crying one moment and laughing the next.

'Do I need my gun?' he says. The grave look on his face makes me laugh until my sides hurt.

★ ★ ★

Fargo lies stretched out on the floor of Gladys's Bar, an empty pitcher near his head, a fleck of foam on his nose. I kneel beside him. A sob flutters in my throat. I run my hand over his head and down his fluffy side. 'Fargo, where have you been?'

His eyes hold a glassy vacancy but he manages to thump his tail and give my chin a nibble. Frack stands behind me, his arms crossed, a smile on his face.

'How did he get here?' I ask.

Wheezy McGee steps forward. He's a grizzled old drunk whose doctor gave him a year to live. He's already outlived the doctor by three. 'He was walking on the side of the road. I remembered him from when you lived upstairs. I whistled and he jumped in the car. Gladys took the hair dryer to him, didn't you Gladys? I got him a bucket of suds. Aside from being too drunk to get up, he's fine.'

'Thank you, Wheezy. I'll never forget this.' I brush away my tears.

'I never seen a cop cry before,' he says.

'Well, don't spread it around, okay?'

'I've never seen a cop in pink pajamas,' says a guy by the pinball machine.

It's obviously time to go before things deteriorate further.

Frack takes a hundred-dollar bill from

his wallet and hands it to Wheezy. His eyes light up. 'For me?' he says.

'Every bit of it,' says Frack. He turns to me. 'Let's get our boy home and get you out of those wet clothes.' He scoops Fargo off the floor and hoists him over his shoulder like a rolled rug. The patrons clap and cheer as we head for the door.

'Thanks, Mom,' I say. 'I really mean that.' I kiss her cheek. She has an expectant look on her face. I almost tell her I love her, but it doesn't happen. It may happen tomorrow. Then again, it may not happen at all.

'Drinks on me!' croaks Wheezy.

'Everyone, belly up to the bar,' says Gladys. 'We've got a lot to celebrate.'

We do hope that you have enjoyed reading this large print book.

Did you know that all of our titles are available for purchase?

We publish a wide range of high quality large print books including:
Romances, Mysteries, Classics
General Fiction
Non Fiction and Westerns

Special interest titles available in large print are:
The Little Oxford Dictionary
Music Book, Song Book
Hymn Book, Service Book

Also available from us courtesy of Oxford University Press:
Young Readers' Dictionary
(large print edition)
Young Readers' Thesaurus
(large print edition)

For further information or a free brochure, please contact us at:
Ulverscroft Large Print Books Ltd.,
The Green, Bradgate Road, Anstey,
Leicester, LE7 7FU, England.
Tel: (00 44) **0116 236 4325**
Fax: (00 44) **0116 234 0205**

Other titles in the
Linford Mystery Library:

THE RETURN OF THE OTHER MRS. WATSON

Michael Mallory

A new collection of puzzlers featuring the second wife of Dr. John H. Watson, of Sherlock Holmes fame. This time Amelia is plunged into a series of affairs that include the case of a carriage that vanishes into thin air, a jewellery theft on board an ocean liner, and an ancient royal document that may challenge the state of the sovereignty itself. As Amelia solves each case with resourcefulness and wit, she demonstrates the Holmesian adage: 'Once you eliminate the impossible, whatever remains, no matter how improbable, must be the truth.'

DARK JOURNEY

Catriona McCuaig

Midwife Maudie Bryant is used to stumbling across murder — but now that she is the mother of a little boy, she has vowed to leave any future crime-solving to her husband Dick, a policeman. However, death strikes too close to home when a wealthy local woman, Cora Beasley, is found strangled with a belt from Maudie's dress. To make matters worse, it is well known that Maudie believed 'the beastly woman was out to snare Dick'. Can Detective Sergeant Bryant help to solve the crime before Maudie is charged as a suspect?

SHERLOCK HOLMES VS. FRANKENSTEIN

David Whitehead

An intriguing mystery lures Sherlock Holmes from the comfort of Baker Street in the winter of 1898: the ghastly murder of a gravedigger in the most bizarre of circumstances. Soon Holmes and Watson are travelling to the tiny German village of Darmstadt, to unmask a callous killer with an even more terrifying motive . . . In nearby Schloss Frankenstein, the eponymous family disowns the rumours attached to its infamous ancestor. But the past cannot be erased, and an old evil is growing strong once again — in the unlikeliest of guises . . .

THE RADIO RED KILLER

Richard A. Lupoff

Veteran broadcaster 'Radio Red' Bob Bjorner is the last of the red-hot lefties working at radio station KRED in Berkeley. His paranoia makes him lock his studio against intruders while he's on the air — but his precaution doesn't save him from a horrible death that leaves him slumped at the microphone just before his three o'clock daily broadcast. Homicide detective Marvia Plum scrambles to the station to investigate. Who amongst the broadcasters, engineers, and administrators present at the station was the murderer — and why?

THE BIG FELLOW

Gerald Verner

Young Inspector Jim Holland of Scotland Yard is under particular pressure to bring to justice 'The Big Fellow' — the mastermind behind a gang committing ever more audacious outrages. As the newspapers mount virulent attacks on Scotland Yard for failing to deal with the rogues, and the crimes escalate from robbery to brutal murder, Holland finds not only his own life threatened, but also that of his theatre actress girlfriend, Diana Carrington.